"Do you get to have toys?"

Unfortunately for Gail's peace of mind, Lily wasn't finished with her questions about Amish life. Gail lifted her daughter onto her hip.

"Okay. Time to go, Lily."

But Samuel's lips twitched with a smile. "Yes, we have toys. But they're Amish toys and might be a little different than you're used to."

Starting to turn away, Gail paused when Lily reached out her hands to bracket Samuel's lean cheeks. "I'm going to call you my Amiss man."

Samuel's white teeth were evident in the smile that stretched between her little hands. "I'm honored, Lily."

With a stiff smile, Gail said goodbye and hustled out of the house and across to the truck. Hurriedly, she buckled Lily into her car seat. As she rounded the front of the truck, she waved an arm to Samuel, who'd stepped out of the house. Gail needed to get going. Before she did something foolish, like echoing that she'd like to call him her Amish man, too.

Growing up on a farm, **Jocelyn McClay** enjoyed livestock and pursued a degree in agriculture. She met her husband while weight lifting in a small town—he "spotted" her. After thirty years in business management, they moved to an acreage in southeastern Missouri to be closer to family when their eldest of three daughters made them grandparents. When not writing, she keeps busy hiking, bike riding, gardening, knitting and substitute teaching.

Books by Jocelyn McClay

Love Inspired

The Amish Bachelor's Choice
Amish Reckoning

Visit the Author Profile page at Harlequin.com.

Amish Reckoning

Jocelyn McClay

LOVE INSPIRED
INSPIRATIONAL ROMANCE

LOVE INSPIRED®
INSPIRATIONAL ROMANCE

Recycling programs
for this product may
not exist in your area.

ISBN-13: 978-1-335-55360-7

Amish Reckoning

For questions and comments about the quality of this book,
please contact us at CustomerService@Harlequin.com.

Love Inspired
22 Adelaide St. West, 40th Floor
Toronto, Ontario M5H 4E3, Canada
www.Harlequin.com

Printed in U.S.A.

Casting all your care upon him;
for he careth for you.
—*1 Peter* 5:7

Always, thanks to God for this opportunity. Thanks to Audra and Moriah for your candid and heartfelt input on sisterhood. Oldest grandchild Judah, you are a precocious inspiration. Lorelle and Debi, your valued feedback improved the story. Kevin, you showed me that romance can be as simple as reading my first novel when I was traveling because you missed me. And Genna, here's to treasured Wednesday chats.

Chapter One

Today was going to change his life. The certainty thrummed through Samuel Schrock as he looked over the farmyard in the predawn darkness of the July morning.

A pinpoint of light pricked the horizon. The muted rumble of a large engine climbing a hill was an odd accompaniment to the growing whistles and calls of waking birds. Samuel stepped off the porch and rubbed his hands together. It was finally happening. He'd longed for this opportunity his whole life.

Smiling wryly, he acknowledged that twenty-two years might not be much of a lifetime according to some of the long-bearded elders in his Amish community. But for Samuel, it seemed like forever since his earliest memory—playing around the legs of his *daed*'s tall Standardbred, an adventure that

almost got him kicked for his enthusiasm—
instilled in him a love of horses.

Earning a living working with them had
been his dream ever since.

When he and younger *bruder*, Gideon,
had moved to Wisconsin to join their eldest
bruder at the furniture business Malachi
had purchased last fall, Samuel figured the
dream would be put on hold while they estab-
lished themselves in a new community. But
thanks to the savvy of the operation's previous owner, Schrock Brothers' Furniture was
already humming along successfully.

It just had one less Schrock brother working in it.

Watching the headlights' steady approach,
Samuel strode to the top of the lane. To the
east, a seam of gold heralded the sun's arrival,
promising a beautiful day. Of course, today
could be pouring down rain, and it would still
be beautiful to him.

The engine picked up speed. Its rumble
would probably wake up Gideon when it
pulled into the yard. *Ach*, well. His *bruder*
would survive. Those in the barn were already up. If the livestock had minded being
fed a little early this morning, as Samuel had
been awake for hours, they'd kept it to themselves.

Malachi agreed to let Samuel leave Schrock Brothers' earlier than anticipated when old Elam Chupp retired from procuring horses for Miller's Creek and other small Amish communities in the region. Kicked one too many times, Elam had explained, but it'd been said with a smile. Samuel had swiftly arranged to take over the business.

He loved his big brother dearly, but he'd lived his whole life in Malachi's shadow. Now was his chance to break free. Earn his way, both economically and psychologically. Prove that he was more than just the charming Schrock brother.

The glow of light split into two separate beams. Samuel retraced his steps to the porch. He didn't want to look too eager, too excited, too inexperienced. The outline of a pickup and a gooseneck trailer approached on the country road.

He'd hired the freight hauler Elam had used and recommended. Gale someone. According to Elam, the hauler was reliable and fair priced, the latter particularly important as margins on sales were slim. Samuel had inquired about other freight outfits and found them to be too expensive for his fledgling business to handle. Elam also said this carrier was decent company, a factor as the Milwaukee racetrack and other locations they'd travel to might be some distance away. Hence the early start.

The truck slowed, presumably looking for addresses as many of the Amish farms in the area looked similar with their big white barns and houses with no electric line connections. Remaining on the porch, Samuel waved an arm, unsure if the driver could see him. The pickup's blinker came on. It turned into the lane.

Watching the truck's approach, Samuel recalled Elam's surprising principle advice. The older man had cautioned that trust—not a good eye for horseflesh or the ability to drive a hard bargain—was the biggest part of the job. Samuel sucked in a deep breath of the early-morning air. Folks had always liked him. He was aware, though, that there was a disparity between liking someone versus trusting and respecting them. Thoughtfully exhaling, Samuel pondered the difference. He didn't anticipate any issue bridging that gap. There wasn't any reason folks shouldn't trust him. He was a man of his word.

Samuel raised an eyebrow as the rig made a circle in the farmyard. Not what he was expecting, although he didn't know why he'd assumed the outfit would be brand-new. It wasn't. The black quad-cab Dodge Ram, although certainly robust enough to handle the gooseneck trailer behind it, had been on the road a number of years. As had the trailer. But both looked in good working condition and were free of rust. Trailer rust and the potential resulting holes were deadly in hauling four-legged animals.

His other brow rose when the driver opened the door and descended from the cab. Well, that would teach him to make assumptions. Apparently, Gale was Gail. There was no mistaking the tall, trim figure encased in jeans and a long-sleeve shirt, or the curly brunette ponytail swinging at the back of her head as anything but female.

Or the pitch of her voice when she asked warily, "Samuel Schrock?"

"Ja." Samuel stepped off the porch, anticipating the smile that always greeted him when he met a woman. This one frowned. She looked disappointed.

The reaction was a new one for him. Bemused, he offered his hand, something Amish didn't normally do, but was a common custom among the *Englisch*. After a moment's hesitation, she reached out her slender one and clasped his for a single brief shake before snatching her hand back and sliding it down the front of her jeans like she was trying to wipe off something distasteful. Samuel blinked. He'd expected numerous new experiences today. But a woman finding him repulsive hadn't been one of them.

He wasn't upset that Gail was female. Women drivers passed him all the time on the road. Though they whipped by his buggy as fast as men—turning to gawk just as frequently, except for the ones who were on their phones in some manner as they drove—he had no issue with them. He was just surprised to see this one climb out of the robust pickup. She looked younger than he was.

But she had a problem with him for some reason. Women, particularly young ones, never had problems with him. Usually it was the other way around.

They stared at each other across a few feet of gravel in the farmyard. Him, with a friendly smile on his face. Her, with anything but. From the chicken coop, a rooster crowed, apparently deciding it was light enough to get about the day's business. At the sound, Gail started, apparently deciding the same thing.

"Get whatever stuff you need and put it in the back of the cab." She pivoted and reached for the door handle.

Samuel found himself facing her swinging ponytail. When she climbed into the cab without looking back, he shrugged. As his notebook, pen and bishop-approved cell phone were in his pocket, he headed for the passenger seat. Rounding the front end of the Dodge, he glanced through the windshield to where Gail already sat on the driver's side. Her expression looked like she'd taken a bite of a fruit, expecting an apple and finding a lemon instead. Samuel sighed softly at the reality that a pretty girl didn't always mean a pretty disposition. It could be a long ride to Milwaukee.

But not if he could help it. She was still female. He was good with women. Whatever issue she might think she had with him, he'd charm her out of it. Opening the door, he entered the truck and buckled himself in.

Shifting in the seat, he faced her now-solemn profile with its delicate brow and dainty nose. Particularly intriguing was the graceful shell of her ear outlined by hair pulled back into a high ponytail, a sight he didn't often see. Frequently, Amish women's ears were at least partially covered by their *kapps*.

"Elam told me about you, but there were some obvious things he left out," Samuel cajoled.

Instead of the flirtatious response he expected, he got a muttered, "He didn't tell me enough about you."

It was a start. "I can tell you more, if you like."

"That's okay." Gail quickly dismissed his offer as she reached for the key in the dash. The engine roared to life. She shifted into gear and the truck started down the lane. As they rolled past the white painted posts of the farm's fence, a grin creased Samuel's cheeks, his companion's perplexing attitude temporarily set aside.

It had begun. His new adventure. His new job. This was his chance to make his life's dream work. To prove himself as more than just a younger brother. And he would do everything in his control to make it successful.

They weren't even out of the lane and Gail was already missing Elam. When he'd announced someone else was taking over his horse-trading business, she'd been expecting an Amish man like him. One wearing a gray beard of some length, indicating he'd been married for years. Slightly homely. Shorter than she was. Sweet. Not charming. Not attractive.

This one made the Ram's cab feel like it had shrunk to the size of a fifty-five-gallon drum, and all the air had been sucked out of it. He made her feel small. And female.

A betraying warmth started in her cheeks and journeyed from there down to her toes in her worn work boots. The long-sleeve shirt she'd donned due to the cool morning now stuck to her flushed skin. Slanting a look at her passenger, she resented that he was so attractive he made her sweat. She cracked the driver's window, causing her ponytail to flutter in the breeze. Bonnie's air-conditioning system had been finicky lately. Gail didn't want to push her luck with it now when she'd need it later in the heat of the afternoon. She prayed that the old pickup wouldn't leave them sweltering.

"Gonna be a warm one today." Her passenger's rich baritone rolled through the cab.

His alluring voice was as disconcerting as his appearance. Gail clicked on the radio. Pop music blasted over the rumble of the engine and the wind's rush through the window, making it difficult to hear. Therefore, difficult to talk. All the better.

They were both slung forward against their seat belts when she braked hard at the stop sign to the highway. It was a good thing there were no horses in the trailer yet. They'd have been knocked off their feet and possibly injured. The thought churned her stomach.

She smoothly pulled onto the pavement. *Get a grip, Gail. Or you won't have to worry about how much you don't want to be around him. He'll take his business elsewhere, and then where will you be?*

Not in a good place. More broke than she was now. She needed this job. She'd been sick with worry when Elam announced he was retiring. The Amish hauls were critical in helping extremely frayed ends meet, especially with fall and the closing of the track for the winter approaching. Gail had already missed one payment on the truck and trailer when the Amish hauls stopped during the business transition. If she missed another payment, she'd lose her rig. The only jobs available to her with an eighth-grade education—waitressing, clerking and other part-time jobs—would barely support her.

On her own, she might be able to survive, but not with Lily. Gail had worked too hard to make it this far. No charming young Amish man, too attractive for his broad-fall britches, was going to upend her life.

Again.

Since he was her customer, a desperately needed one, Gail tipped her head toward the dash and raised her voice to be heard over the chirpy female one coming through the speakers. "Do you mind the music?"

He grinned at her across what had once seemed like a wide seat and shouted back, "No, not at all."

Gail faced forward again, eyes on the road in front of her, resenting his charming smile.

He looked like a younger version of an actor. The big, brawny blond one who carried a hammer in the superhero movies she'd watched on her streaming service, the one perk her meager budget allowed. He should look ridiculous—Samuel, not the actor—but he didn't.

He wore a flat-brimmed straw hat, suspenders, dark blue pants and work boots. His hair was a little shorter and cut differently than the long bowl style normally worn by Amish men. That indicated he was in his *rumspringa*, when a few more liberties were allowed. The sun-lined creases bracketing his crinkling blue eyes indicated the charming smile was frequently in place. Eyes that were about the same blue as the awakening sky beyond the windshield.

She despised blue eyes. She despised charming young Amish men. Blond ones were the worst. Shifting on the cloth seat,

Gail scowled. He was attractive. She was attracted. Therefore, he was off-limits, as she'd proved herself a lousy judge of character with attractive men. Besides, it didn't matter to her. It couldn't. Because he was Amish. And she wasn't.

Not anymore.

And although she longed to, she couldn't go back. Not if she was going to keep her daughter.

A muffled boom merged with the reverberating percussion of the music and rush of the wind through the lowered window. The steering wheel jerked and began vibrating, pulling hard toward the side of the road. Gail tightened her grip like she was trying to hold on to a wild animal instead of a circle of plastic. Instantly nauseated at what it meant, Gail flicked on her blinker and let up on the gas. When she noted the intersection for a country road, she puffed out a breath in relief. Turning cautiously onto it, she pulled the truck off to the side and shut it down. In the ensuing silence, broken only by the cooling tick of the engine, she slumped back against the seat and closed her eyes.

"Oh, Bonnie. How could you do this to me? I was going to take care of you," she muttered. "You were supposed to last just a little longer."

"Is everything all right?"

No. Far from it. Opening her eyes, she glanced at Samuel and forced a smile, hoping it didn't look as sour as her stomach felt. "It'll be fine."

Although his brow furrowed, he seemed satisfied with her assurance. "You named the truck? We name our animals, but—" his eyes bounced around the cab's interior "—this is a piece of metal."

Not to Gail it wasn't. All her hopes, dreams and sacrifices were tied up in the truck and the trailer behind it. Her and her daughter's future were literally riding on the Dodge's wheels. One of which was now most assuredly flat. As was her bank account, which couldn't afford to replace it or the other three of matching condition.

At the moment, her too-attractive passenger was the least of her worries.

Chapter Two

With a heavy sigh, Gail set the parking brake, unbuckled and climbed from the truck. Pushing the door shut, she found the bottom third of the truck's front wheel level with the road surface. Her shoulders sagged in relief when it looked like the rim had escaped damage. Gail strode to the back of the truck to get the spare tire.

She'd feared this was coming. She'd been pressing a penny into the truck tires for the last month, wishing that somehow Lincoln's hairstyle would morph into something tall enough to reach the shrinking treads. Gail knew the tires wouldn't make it through winter, but she'd hoped they'd at least make it into the fall before she needed to spend money she didn't have.

Gail blinked back a threat of tears. *Gott*

would provide. He always had. She just wished she didn't have to be such a nuisance to Him.

Dropping the tailgate, Gail reached for the spare, only to see work-calloused hands grab hold of it first.

"I got it."

Samuel's arm brushed her shoulder. Gail's startled inhalation caught a whiff of soap and the pleasant musk of horses. Hastily stepping back, she bumped her head on the gooseneck of the trailer. It made less of an impact to her equilibrium than finding herself the focus of Samuel's blue eyes and dazzling smile.

"I knew this day would be full of new adventures. Just didn't expect them to start before we got to the track." Lifting the tire from the truck bed, he added, "We can't leave Bonnie here lingering with a broken leg." He nodded toward the flat tire. "What do you use to lift the truck?"

"I'll get the jack." Gail ducked under the gooseneck, dashed to the front passenger door and uncovered the jack assembly. When she turned in the V of the open truck door, he was there. She held the jack in front of her like a shield. It wasn't much protection against her escalating heartbeat that hammered away at his nearness. "Got it," she said unnecessarily.

To her relief, he stepped back and she skirted around him to the tire, pulled off the hubcap and began setting up the jack. Seconds later Samuel crouched at her shoulder.

He was too much like the Amish charmer she'd fallen for years ago, too close for her ricocheting senses and too tempting for her obvious poor judgment in men.

"Do you…ah…know what it is to block a wheel?"

Samuel smiled at her as if she'd asked if he knew what shoofly pie was. "*Ja*, I think I can handle that."

"Can you block the far rear one?" The errand would give her a moment of space. Working quickly, she had the jack in place and the nuts loosened by the lug wrench. Gail was starting to loosen the nuts the rest of the way manually when Samuel's fingers reached for the next lug nut and their hands brushed. Gail jerked hers back. As he quickly loosened that one and moved on to the next, she dropped the nut she held into the upturned hubcap with a clang and stood.

The remaining bolts were quickly stripped of lug nuts under his capable fingers. Samuel pulled the flat tire off and set it aside. "It's pretty much like changing a buggy wheel—" he grunted as he lifted the spare onto the bolts

"—except with rubber, heavier, wider and the buggy has a name." He shot her a grin over his shoulder. "Where'd you come up with *Bonnie*?"

"Ah." Gail wasn't going to mention that Bonnie, a big Percheron mare, had been her favorite among her *daed*'s draft horses. "Um, black truck. *Bonnie* starts with *B*. Just popped into my head when I was driving." *One time when I was traveling long miles by myself, trying to support a child, so homesick I cried for about sixty miles. I just needed something from home.*

Gail slid the hubcap with the lug nuts within his reach. Grabbing the deflated tire, she maneuvered it to the truck's tailgate, wrestled it into the bed and slammed the tailgate shut. Samuel had stepped back from the wheel by the time she returned. Kneeling, Gail released the jack and used the wrench to finish tightening the nuts.

"I can do that." Samuel's voice came from just off her shoulder.

Gail switched the wrench to the next nut, her brow lowering as she stared at the tread of the spare. It wasn't in much better condition than the flat they'd removed. Reality settled in like the weight of the truck on the unjacked tire. "I got it. My truck, my responsibility. But thanks for your help." He must have heard the dismissal in her tone, as he stepped aside. Gail could feel his gaze on the back of her head.

Concern for her and Lily's future chased away the long-dormant feelings of awareness and attraction that'd fluttered like a newly caged bird through her. She had no time for such frivolous things when their livelihood was at risk. Without another word, she stored the jack assembly, leaving the front passenger door open in unspoken invitation for him to get into the truck. As she rounded the hood, Gail glanced dejectedly at the other front tire, apprehensive now that it'd blow out as well before they reached the city. She'd let it go too far. They all needed replacing. There was no more postponing the inevitable.

With slumped shoulders, she climbed into the truck. Returning to the highway inter-section after finding a lane in which to turn around, Gail looked to the right and found Samuel watching her. Giving him a weak, warped smile, she turned on the radio again. Upbeat music, contradictory to her mood, re-verberated through the cab as she pulled onto the road.

As they headed toward Milwaukee, Gail didn't know which was more detrimental to her peace of mind—the attractive Amish man beside her or her nonexistent finances that were about to get worse.

Finances won. With risky tires, she couldn't make any income. Without the income, she'd lose the rig. Without the rig—Gail inhaled sharply through her nose—she could lose her daughter.

When Samuel asked a few questions, Gail cranked the music to avoid conversation and the distraction it brought. Hands firm on the steering wheel in case another of Bonnie's tires decided to go, she sent up a simple prayer. *Gott* said not to worry about tomorrow, but that was hard to remember when your future was riding on four bald tires and an empty bank account.

Unfortunately for her bank account, but fortunately for the sorry turn of events, Gail had no extra hauls scheduled that day. At the track, she took a moment to introduce Samuel to a few key people, primarily trainer George Hayes, before leaving the trailer in the track's back parking lot and heading for the tire dealer George had recommended.

Safety first. The thought drummed through her head in concert with her fingers that rested on the open window. Her daughter was an occasional passenger. Her reputation transporting horses depended on it. Gail's heart pounded at the possibility of a blowout and loss of control when Lily was in the truck, or an equine passenger was in the trailer.

She could live without air-conditioning. She had for years growing up. She couldn't live without safe tires. Getting a complete set was the right thing to do. Even knowing that truth, her stomach twisted as later she handed over the credit card that already had a balance higher than her bank account.

She'd have to get an extra job. Gail's stomach wrenched further. That would mean more missed time with her three-year-old daughter. It felt like she was rarely home as it was.

Home. Gail flattened her lips at the thought of it. Not the tiny basement apartment she shared with Lily, but the well-kept farm Gail had grown up on. If only she could go home…

Picking up the newspaper in the waiting area, she flipped to the want ads. There were jobs, but nothing she was qualified for. Gail dropped the paper and crossed her arms. Hopefully, Samuel knew what he was doing and was more than just a pretty face. Although Gail made some money with him as a passenger, the real money was when she was hauling horses. If he bought even one or, better yet, two today, it would help her desperate finances. She'd be thrilled enough to ignore her hard-earned wariness and hug Samuel Schrock's handsome neck.

If he'd only buy a horse.

Samuel waited outside George Hayes's stable block where Gail had left him that morning.

It'd been a *wunderbar* day. Knowing that he looked strange even for a stranger, Samuel had been uncharacteristically nervous when he'd first arrived at the track, but the few brief introductions from Gail had set him on an effective course for the day. He'd even bought a horse, an older gelding that no longer made the time trials, from George. It was a risk on his first day, but Gail obviously respected the older man, so Samuel figured it was safe to do so, as well.

He smiled at the thought of his freight hauler. Old Elam must've had something he didn't, because if Gail was what Elam called decent company, the man hadn't gotten out much. Or had spent too much time with only horses.

Of course, maybe she didn't get out much, either, if she was naming her truck. He snorted at the memory. Samuel almost wished there'd been four tires needing changing instead of just the one. She'd seemed almost friendly there by the side of the road.

But as soon as they'd climbed back into the truck, it was back to business and ear-ringing music. Samuel liked *Englisch* music, but he liked a good conversation, as well. Particularly one with a pretty woman. With her dark hair and expressive blue eyes, Gail-the-freight-hauler was definitely a pretty woman.

One who was as skittish around him as an unbroken filly. Old Elam had indicated that trust was paramount in his new position, but Samuel had never figured that would be an issue with women. He'd never had a problem with them before, Amish or *Englisch*. He didn't expect one now, but it was hard to flirt with a woman while shouting. And every effort of his had been deflected. The woman certainly had a way with words. A way of speaking as few of them as possible.

The July afternoon sun beat down on him. Using a knuckle to tip his flat-brimmed hat farther back off his sweating forehead, Samuel watched the horse and the human traffic that flowed around him. It was quieter in the stable block now than it'd been earlier. A number of equine athletes were already returned to their stalls for the day. Latecomers from the track passed, some with jog carts, most with racing bikes; their nickers of greeting to their stablemates along with the stomps of shod hooves, rattle of stall doors and murmur of distant conversations were muffled in the sultry air.

Glancing down the shed row, Samuel caught sight of Gail, immediately recognizable from her long but feminine stride and graceful lean figure. She walked like she had someplace to go and was intent on getting there. His lips curved into an admiring smile. Although he enjoyed the efforts of the young Amish women who'd vied for his favor, none had caught his attention. But this one might. Samuel's smile widened. Then she'd throw it right back at him.

She'd been in the back of his mind all afternoon, which was disconcerting as so many *wunderbar* new things had been peppering the front. His driver was very attractive indeed, but Samuel wasn't about to do anything to risk their professional relationship. He needed Gail for his business. And based on the age of the truck, the trailer and her worn blue jeans, she needed him as a customer.

While it'd been a *gut* day for him, as Gail got closer he could tell from her drooping shoulders that it hadn't been such a *gut* one for her.

She stopped several feet away from him. "Ready?" Distressed or not, she wasn't one to dawdle.

Samuel nodded and tipped his head back toward George's stable block. "Need to pick up a horse first."

"Really?"

For a moment Samuel thought he was seeing a second sunrise in the day, the way Gail's face lit up. She lunged forward, her arms lifted like she was going to throw them around his neck.

Chapter Three

They were inches apart for a breathless moment before Gail took a step back, her face as red as some racing silks that he'd seen on the track that day. Releasing a quiet sigh, Samuel regretted that she hadn't come to her senses a few seconds later.

Samuel knew he'd love this job. And if this was the way his pretty driver reacted when he made a purchase, he envisioned himself quickly gaining a small herd of horses, the big white barn at the farm bursting at the seams.

Gail awkwardly rubbed her hands together. "Let's, ah, let's go get him, then."

Nodding, Samuel turned and headed for the stall that held his new purchase, with Gail falling in step beside him.

"He's a sweetie." Gail ran a hand down the sleek neck of the gelding while Samuel obtained a lead rope from the attending groom. "I can tell by his eyes. They're patient. Approachable. Calm." She smoothed the horse's forelock over the bay's broad forehead.

Samuel suppressed his responding snort. That was at least three qualities the gelding didn't share with the woman petting him. Snapping the lead rope to the horse's halter, he unhooked the half door and led the horse out. "Those characteristics might be the very reasons he's coming with me instead of staying at the track." The steady clip-clop of the bay's steps accompanied them as they headed for the parking lot.

"Different realities in life require different strengths. I'm sure he'll do fine in his new role. You have a prospective buyer for him?"

"I've got a neighbor who mentioned he was looking for a new horse for his wife. I'm thinking this one might be a good fit."

On the other side of the horse, it was quiet a moment before he heard her murmur, "Good. Sometimes it's hard to find the right fit for your life."

When they reached the truck and trailer, the gelding loaded like the pro he was. After watching Gail secure the trailer latch, Samuel walked the length of the trailer, pausing when he reached the rear of the truck and noticed the tires, all dark and shiny.

He raised his voice to be heard across the truck where she was approaching the driver's side. "You didn't just replace the one?"

From the far side of the truck he heard the slam of the cab door. Gail didn't respond until Samuel climbed in beside her. "They all needed to be replaced. It's safer." She gave him a lopsided smile. "Don't want to give our new passenger a ride like this morning." She started the engine and rolled down the windows. "Or worse."

They pulled out of the parking lot, the open windows letting in a hot breeze. As they took the ramp to the interstate, the truck's speed picked up, as did the rush of air into the cab. Although loud, it didn't prohibit conversation like the music had on the way in.

Gail glanced over, frowning apologetically. "Sorry about the windows. The air-conditioning is misbehaving."

Samuel grinned. "S'all right. It's about the only thing I've faced today that I'm used to. At home, instead of the breeze blowing in the side windows, it's coming through the front. And it doesn't come as fast."

He thought her lips tipped up toward a

smile, but he wasn't sure. "Bonnie seems a bit cantankerous."

Gail patted the weathered dash. "She's all right. Just needs a little support and TLC now and then, like all of us."

"Speaking of support, thank you for the introductions this morning."

"No problem." For a few miles, except for the streaming wind noise, it was silent. Samuel saw Gail glance at the radio, like she was thinking of turning it on, but didn't. Instead, she pitched her voice above the cab noise and asked, "Elam didn't mention much about you. Are you originally from the Miller's Creek area?"

"*Nee*. Moved up to Wisconsin from Ohio last year. Followed my older *bruder*." He shrugged. "Seems I'm always following him in some manner. This is my first solo adventure. Malachi's very successful. He's…" Samuel struggled with words that would accurately describe his *bruder*. "I admire him greatly, but it's time for me to strike my own path. That's why this job opportunity is *wunderbar*. It's a chance to make my own way doing something I love." He rested an elbow on the edge of the open window. "You ever feel like a sapling under the shade of a huge oak tree?"

Samuel glanced over at Gail. Her mouth was slightly open, as if she was about to say something, but all the conversation was in her eyes. It must have been a difficult one. Samuel didn't speak, waiting to hear what she wanted to share. When she remained silent, he took pity on her.

"What? No music this time?" To him, it was a victory. The comment earned him another small smile.

Gail clicked on the radio and adjusted it so it was just a quiet thrum under the sound of the breeze. Her shoulders rose and fell under a slow, deep sigh. "So what does your oak of a brother do?"

Samuel grinned at the reference. It was an apt description of Malachi. "He owns a furniture business. A shop and the attached store in Miller's Creek. Used to be Fisher Furniture."

Gail remembered Fisher Furniture. It'd been a fixture on Miller's Creek's main street. She used to love going into town on shopping day. "What happened to the Fishers?"

"Amos Fisher died sometime back. Don't know the cause, but he'd apparently been sick awhile. Bishop Weaver wouldn't allow his daughter to continue to own the shop that employed several men, so she had to sell. Malachi bought the business and a farm—the one you picked me up at this morning—and we moved in."

Gail's fingers tightened on the wheel as she recalled her own encounters with the Weaver family. She wasn't surprised to hear Bishop Weaver had forced another Amish community member into something against their wishes.

From her peripheral vision, Gail could see that Samuel was smiling. He always seemed to be smiling. Didn't the man take anything seriously? "What?" she pressed when he didn't say any more.

"In the move, Malachi ended up with the business and a wife. He married the previous owner's daughter. I'm not sure how that happened. Most of their interactions that I witnessed had her fluffed up like an outraged cat. But one day she was making arrangements to leave the community and seems like the next, their upcoming wedding was announced in church."

Gail remembered Ruth Fisher, as well. She was glad for her. She'd always liked the energetic Ruth. Glancing over at her passenger, she found Samuel watching her pensively, like he was going to ask her something. Possibly something about her own history.

That wasn't going to happen.

"So, what? You flunked at making tables, chairs and dressers?"

"If *flunk* is the same as *fail*, I didn't flunk at anything. Not to be *hochmut*, but I was a pretty good furniture maker."

Gail's own lips twitched at the wry grin on his handsome face.

"Most of the time," he conceded. He shifted in his seat, turning more to face her. "Ruth caught occasional, very minor—" he held his fingers a hairbreadth apart "—errors and made me correct them. When they were married, they moved to Ruth's farm. With settling into the farm, the furniture business and now a new wife, my *bruder* has his hands full. One of the reasons that Malachi released me from the business was that I'm taking on more of the farmwork for both places. I'm *gut* with that. My *bruder* is a fair boss, but I'd rather be working outside and with livestock instead of being under a roof all day."

That was something Gail easily understood. She missed being part of a working farm. The baby animals in the spring. The warm earth beneath her bare feet in the garden. Lily would've loved those and other aspects of a close-knit family farm life. If only they could go home…

"So who's your oak?"

Although Gail's eyes were on the road and the sweeping Wisconsin countryside, her older sister immediately came to mind. She hadn't talked about her family to anyone in years. The vehicle slowed as a tsunami of homesickness swept over her. Glancing over, Gail found Samuel watching her again. There was no judgment in his gaze. Only a speck of…commiseration? She returned her attention to the highway in front of her.

"My sister. She's perfect. Never puts a foot wrong no matter the situation." The words escaped before she realized it. Puffing out a breath, Gail continued, "Which was the opposite of me growing up. I was more impulsive, which sometimes got me in trouble." She frowned. "I'd like to despise her perfection, but in addition to being perfect, she's…sweet. Really nice. Sincerely nice."

Recollections of her older sister made Gail swallow hard. She shot a look at Samuel again. He was nodding his head solemnly, as if he understood.

"*Ach*, I see what you mean. She isn't like you at all."

Gail blinked and dropped her jaw as she processed what he'd said. Without thinking, she reached out and bumped his shoulder with her fist. He didn't try to dodge, just grinned his magical grin.

"So how did you become such a fine, sturdy tree, then?" There was humor in his voice, but all thoughts of responding to its playful timbre evaporated from Gail at the memory of how she'd had to change so much, so fast.

"I moved away." Leaning forward, she flicked up the volume on the radio. "And never went back."

To her dismay, he reached out and turned it back down. "Why not?"

Gail strove to ignore the warmth that ran up her spine at the rich tone of his voice. She attributed it to the thought of revealing her history. Wasn't going to happen. An expert in redirection, she responded, "I'd always heard that men liked to talk about themselves."

Although her eyes were fixed on the windshield in front of her, she could hear the smile in his voice. "You must be thinking of *Englisch* men. It would be too *hochmut* for an Amish man to do so."

Gail snorted. "And you aren't proud?" There was an unexpected silence where she'd expected a quick retort.

His voice was thoughtful when he finally responded. "Not *hochmut*. Just…confident.

Sometimes it takes confidence to get things done. To face new situations. If I didn't have some level of confidence, how could I have the courage to leave my old job and start a new, uncertain one?"

Gail pulled off the highway onto the country road that led to his farm. She was surprised at his insight. If she hadn't had some level of confidence in herself, she'd never have made it as a pregnant teenager leaving the Amish community. It had tested every minute amount she'd had. Still did.

She'd already succumbed once to a charming Amish man. Look where that'd gotten her. While she couldn't afford to lose this man as a customer, she couldn't afford any attraction to him. Gail tightened her grip on the steering wheel. As long as Samuel limited his obvious passion to his job and not his driver, they wouldn't have a problem.

Slowing for the turn into his lane, she glanced toward the big white house. What she saw in the farmyard drove the breath from her body.

Climbing into a buggy were two women, one petite with auburn hair, the other tall and blonde.

Hissing in a breath, Gail made the careful turn off the road and pulled to the edge of the

two-track gravel lane. Not wanting to stop—
that might prompt the approaching buggy to
do so, as well—she kept the truck inching
along as far to the side of the driveway as she
could. Blindly, she flipped up the armrest beside her and dug in between the seats until she
closed her fingers on the brim of her ball cap.
Snatching it, with one hand still clenched on
the steering wheel, she awkwardly tugged it
on, pulling the brim as low on her forehead
as possible. Whipping her head toward the
pasture that bordered the lane, she tried fo-
cusing her gaze on the two placid Belgians
grazing there, only to see Samuel watching
her, a puzzled frown on his face.

"It's my sister-in-law, Ruth, and her friend
Hannah Lapp. Every once in a while they
take pity on my younger *bruder*, Gideon, and
me and bring over some food. Unfortunately,
they draw the line at housecleaning and doing
laundry. They've seen female *Englisch* drivers before. Don't worry."

He lifted a hand to wave. Gail captured
his hand, surprising them both. Jerking hers
back, Gail grabbed the wheel with both hands.
Unrestrained, Samuel gave a friendly wave
to the pair, his eyes remaining on Gail. His
look said he probably thought she was jeal-
ous. *Let him*. It was the least of her concerns.

Gail glanced up the lane. From the corner of her eye, she saw the two women wave back. Beneath the *kapps* whose ribbons floated in the breeze of the moving buggy, Gail could easily make out their smiling faces. Hunching her shoulders, she sank lower in the seat. When the two vehicles were side by side, she put her hand by her face, ducked her head and stared at the footwell under Samuel's seat. Breathing shallowly, she could hear the clip-clop of hooves and the buggy wheels crunching on gravel as they passed a few feet away. *Please don't stop, please don't stop...* The mantra echoed in her head as she counted the eyelets on his brown work boots.

The truck inched forward. When the sounds of the rig faded, Gail dragged in a deep breath.

"They're gone."

Lifting her head, Gail checked the rearview mirror to ensure the buggy wasn't turning around. Only when their Standardbred sprang into a ground-covering trot did her anxiety ebb. Silently, she drove up the rest of the lane and circled the farmyard to back the trailer toward the barn. Shifting into Park, she reluctantly faced Samuel.

His eyes were hooded. "Do you have a problem with Amish women? The choices they've made? Maybe they don't have the liberties you do in the *Englisch* world. But it's a noble life."

Now dizzy with relief, Gail shook her head. No, she had no problem with Amish women. She'd intended to be one. She'd planned to take her place in the Amish community. But sometimes life changed course on you.

The Belgians in the pasture welcomed the newcomer with a chorus of neighs, which he energetically returned from the trailer, jolting her back from the past. "No problem. I just need to get your horse unloaded so I can get back on the road."

Never before had she unloaded a horse so quickly. Usually, she loved an opportunity to explore big Amish barns, but not today. As she drove down the lane ten minutes later, Gail tugged off the cap, tossing it on the passenger seat. Her head flopped back against the headrest. Yes, she had a problem with those women. One in particular. The blonde one. She was the most beautiful Amish woman Gail had ever seen.

Her older sister hadn't changed at all.

Chapter Four

The empty trailer rattled down the lane. Hands on his hips, Samuel watched the truck turn and accelerate down the country road. She was going faster than normal. What'd upset her?

Returning to the shadowed interior of the barn, he unhooked the halter and tugged the lead free from where he'd hastily tied the gelding in a stall when he realized the clanking that'd followed him into the barn was Gail securing the door of the trailer at lightning speed. By the time he'd reached the double doors of the barn, she was pulling out.

He'd wanted to say farewell. *Ach*, more so, he'd wanted to probe a little about her strange reaction when Ruth and Hannah passed them in the lane. The usual *Englisch* response when they saw Amish was either to stare outright or pretend they weren't when they really were. Perhaps Gail had worked with Elam so long and delivered enough horses to his farm that she had a more nonchalant response? But her actions had been anything but disinterested. She'd almost slunk all the way to the floorboards. He doubted she could see over the dash as the truck crept up the lane.

Gail didn't seem to have a problem with him. Well, she had a problem with him but not in that way. Maybe she had an issue with strangers? If she had, she was capable of getting over it, as the folks at the track appeared to like her well enough.

His new purchase wandered around the unfamiliar stall, nosing the fresh straw cushioning the floor. Samuel hooked the stall door closed. Ascending the ladder to the hayloft, he dropped down a fresh bale. When he climbed back down, his mare, Belle, and the new gelding were eyeing him with interest.

He snorted at their avid attention, the dust motes kicked up by the dropped bale swirling about him. "Too bad women aren't as easy to understand as you two. I can tell by your ears what you want." Unbidden, the vision of Gail's ears under her high ponytail sprang into his mind. Samuel tripped over the bale as he went to get the knife that hung on the barn wall to cut the twine. Quickly recovering, he glanced sheepishly back to the watching bays.

"You don't mind a quiet conversation instead of a loud radio." He snorted again. "You answer about the same amount of questions. In fact, I probably know as much or more of your history, even upon our short acquaintance, than I do hers." Samuel rubbed the gelding's forehead when the horse reached over the stall wall to lip some loose hay from his shirt.

Bending, Samuel cut the twine from the bale. It relaxed into an accordion of separate flakes, releasing a strong scent of fresh-cut hay.

"I'd like to say I like you better for your straightforwardness. But I don't want to lie. There's just something…" Samuel breathed in the sweet hay aroma, one of his favorite smells. He realized, though, as he tossed a few flakes of it into each horse's manger, that a more intriguing one now was the clean soap fragrance that'd greeted him this morning when he climbed into the truck's cab with Gail. Samuel frowned as he straightened up the open bale.

"A mysterious woman just makes a man wonder." Ambling over to Belle, he stretched out a hand to scratch her between the ears. She jerked her head up and swung it out of reach, avoiding his touch. Shaking his head, Samuel retreated, giving her space to return to the hay in the manger. "Or maybe I'm just a fool for skittish females."

Turning his back on the mare, he crossed to a large pen in the back of the cavernous barn, vaulted the low gate there and strode through the pen to open the door that exited to an attached pasture. Jeb and Huck, the two Belgians, were waiting just outside. Gabby, the Guernsey cow, wasn't far behind. "It'd be nice if she'd trust me like you all do." Stepping aside as the trio entered the barn, he looked down the road in the direction the truck and trailer had taken. "Something for me to work on, I figure."

Gail hadn't seen Hannah in years. Four, to be exact, when Gail's pregnancy was getting too difficult to hide. The day her folks were gone to an auction, when she'd walked down the lane with her eyes full of tears and her hands full of the few possessions she could carry to the bus stop.

Hannah had followed her to the road, her normally pristine apron wadded in clenched fists, trying to convince Gail to stay. But after a lingering final embrace, Gail had started walking. She hadn't looked back.

With only an eighth-grade education, as per Amish practice, even part-time jobs for her were scarce. Somehow she'd ended up at the racetrack and *Gott* had answered her fervent prayers. Standardbred trainer George Hayes had needed a stable hand. Or maybe George hadn't. Maybe he'd just known that Gail desperately needed a job. He gave her one.

She'd learned to drive, as a license didn't require a high school diploma and it was something she could do while roundly pregnant. She'd scrimped together enough to put a small down payment on Bonnie and the trailer. Although the years since had been tough, she thought they'd finally be able to make it.

Until she hit a rough patch and missed some payments.

Scouring the rural area she traveled in for cheaper rent and childcare, *Gott* had again answered Gail's prayers when she found a widow with a small basement apartment who was thrilled to watch Lily during the day. The downside was its proximity to Miller's Creek. If the wrong person found out about Lily, she risked losing her daughter. But if Gail couldn't keep a roof over their heads, she could lose her anyway. And that would happen if the truck and trailer were repossessed.

She'd worried Elam would recognize her. When he didn't say anything, Gail allowed herself a sliver of hope. Later in conversation he admitted that he didn't pay a lot of attention to the *youngies* and she breathed easier, casually probing him for news of home. That was how she learned about the death of Atlee Weaver, Lily's father.

No. No one from Miller's Creek could know she was nearby.

The buggy had fortunately turned down another road. Gail stopped at the intersection, shifting into Park. Crossing her wrists over the top of the steering wheel, she dropped her forehead against them.

She missed her family.

Seeing Hannah was like having a swollen river top a levee and weaken it, threatening to wash away the whole protective barrier.

She wanted to go home.

Gail raised her head at the sound of a passing car. Her eyes blinking back tears, she considered the roads before her. If she turned one way, it led to the small town where she lived. If she turned another…it would take her down the country road that led to her family's farm.

Shifting the truck into gear, Gail turned on the country road and drove by well-remembered territory.

Her pulse started throbbing when her family's white-painted buildings topped the landscape. *I'm not going to turn my head to look as I pass. Too much like* Englisch *gawkers.* Even so, the truck slowed to a crawl when she reached the beginning of her *daed*'s property, as Gail scanned the neat farmyard.

The wash was on the line. Oh my, the pants were getting long. Her younger brothers must be growing so big. Aprons and solid-colored dresses fluttered in the breeze. Dropping a quick glance to her jeans, Gail tried to remember the last time she'd worn a Plain dress.

She dashed a hand across her tear-blurred eyes when she saw the apron-wearing figure in the garden. *Mamm.* Against her resolve, Gail twisted her head, continuing to look as she drove past. A loud blare of a horn had her swerving the pickup back to her side of the road. A driver glared at her through the window of a passing SUV. A tug on the steering wheel warned the wheels of the trailer had dropped into the shallow ditch. She'd lose her livelihood if she tore up her rig. Berating herself, Gail eased the trailer back onto the blacktop surface.

Maybe some church Sunday when she knew they'd be gone, she'd drive by with Lily. Nothing would be said about unknown grandparents, but Gail could point out what a beautiful and carefully maintained farm looked like. Yes, they could do that. Lily would enjoy it and she…she needed to show her.

Did *Mamm* have any grandchildren beside Lily? Surely Hannah was married by now. Or was the reason Hannah was coming over with Ruth to the Schrock farm because she was interested in Samuel?

The truck shot forward with the sudden pressure on the gas pedal. It slowed again when Gail forced her foot to relax. What girl wouldn't be? Gail's stomach twisted as she vividly recalled being second choice for an attractive Amish man before. And the bleak outcome.

Get over him, Gail. She shouldn't be dreaming about an Amish man. If Samuel happened to marry her sister, well…it wasn't like she'd be around to see them together.

She longed to head straight home to where Lily waited for her. But the black-and-white Holsteins in her *daed*'s pasture had reminded her of their milkless refrigerator. She'd intended to grab some groceries while in town, but the flat tire and her new customer had driven everyday things from her mind.

Even with the warm breeze that blew through the open window, a cold sweat broke out over Gail. She couldn't afford to drive the many miles out of the way to another grocery store when there was one almost in her path. If she went into Miller's Creek.

Surely *Gott* had tested her enough today? Surely she could run into a store without seeing someone she knew? The meager amount in her checkbook persuaded her that the odds should be in her favor.

Gail pulled into the small grocery store's parking lot. Her left foot bounced in the footwell when she saw the horse and buggy hitched to the rail made available for Amish customers. She stilled the action with a hand on her leg. *It's not* Mamm *or* Daed. *Hannah wouldn't have had time to get into town. I look different. No one else knows me as well. As long as it isn't... But what are the chances that out of all in the community, it's Ruby Weaver's buggy? The woman probably doesn't do anything as mundane as grocery shopping. She's too busy manipulating lives.*

Retrieving the baseball cap from the passenger seat, she tugged it low on her forehead. With a deep breath, Gail exited the truck and hurried across the parking lot. Slipping through the sliding doors, she ignored the carts and scanned the produce section for anyone wearing a dress and *kapp*. The coast was clear. Exhaling slowly, Gail peeked into the first aisle. Finding it empty, she headed for the back of the store.

Gail flicked her gaze down the aisles as she passed. Clear. Clear. Noting the sign indicating box goods, her breath hitched at the sight of a woman in an aisle until she quickly identified the shopper by attire as *Englisch*. She trotted down it to grab a box of mac and cheese. Returning to the refrigerated coolers at the back of the store, she snagged a package of hot dogs and a gallon of milk. Gail's shoulders relaxed as she rounded the endcap of the last aisle. Just a loaf of bread and she was done. *No one is going to recognize me. It's been four years. I'm an unreasonable coward, except the stakes are so high. But that's only if I see...*

Gail stood motionless, almost as if she'd become one of the items in the hip-high freezer at her side. Atlee's mother, Ruby Weaver, was halfway down the aisle, wearing a frown like a required piece of clothing as she stared at the shelf in front of her. While the years had changed Gail, time hadn't made a difference to Ruby. The belt of her apron sagged at the waist of her gaunt figure. Her *kapp*, pressed in iron folds, was anchored scrupulously to her steel-gray hair. Ruby's eyes were narrowed on the container in her hand, as if she planned to recommend shunning it for offending her in some manner.

It was a look Gail remembered well. An amplified version of it had pinned a sixteen-year-old Gail to a barn wall where Ruby had cornered her alone after the church service announcing Atlee's engagement—to another girl. Calling Gail a jezebel, the bishop's wife warned her to leave her son alone, or Gail would regret it, as would her family.

Later, Gail wished she'd retorted that Ruby's cherished son had been the seducer, probably of many young Amish women, but at the time, she'd been shocked and scared. She still was, because Ruby was the neck that turned the head of the bishop. A bishop who interpreted the community's *Ordnung* in a manner that best suited his own family.

Ruby pivoted and stared unblinkingly at where Gail stood rooted. Ducking her head, Gail stared at the bags of frozen chicken breasts in the freezer, her fingers white-knuckled on the groceries in her hands. *She won't recognize me. The hat. The ponytail, the jeans. It's my imagination that she's watching me. I'm just an* Englisch *girl*. Gail forced herself to move along the far side of the freezer, working her way to the front of the store.

From under the bill of her cap, she sneaked

a glance at the older woman. Ruby's eyes, under the center part of her hair, were hooded as she watched Gail. The older woman's pursed lips gathered up the loose wrinkles from her face. Gail ignored the bread section and hastened to check out. Thrusting her items onto the conveyor belt, she looked back to find the bishop's wife had followed her to the end of the aisle and stood, hands on narrow hips, staring at her.

Foot tapping a rapid tattoo on the tile, Gail waited for her change. When she had it, she grabbed her items and fled the store, feeling a burning stare between her shoulders with every step. Shoving her purchases to the passenger seat, she jumped into the cab. Moments later the truck and trailer rattled out of the parking lot.

Gail was half a mile out of town before her heart rate slowed down. Ruby Weaver was the reason she couldn't return to the Amish community. The threat the bishop's wife posed to her daughter forced Gail and Lily to stay in the *Englisch* world. If Ruby ever found out her precious dead son, Atlee, actually had a daughter, she'd use the bishop to gain custody of the child.

Elam lived on the fringe of the Amish community. Samuel's farm was closer to the center. Somehow, Gail needed to avoid Miller's Creek while supporting her new—and very distracting—customer.

Pulling into the main street of a town so small it couldn't boast a gas station, Gail circled a block and parked the pickup and trailer along a side street lined with small, neat houses.

Grabbing her groceries, Gail shut the door with her hip and headed for the sidewalk. She had greater things to worry about than a man. Yes, Samuel Schrock was tempting, but he didn't fit into her life. And he didn't hold a candle to what did. Gail smiled as she crossed bright-colored chalk marks on the cement pavement, the tension of the day easing from her shoulders at the unidentifiable drawings. Before she reached the screen door, it flew open and a small blond-haired girl bounded down the steps and launched into her arms.

"Mommy! You're here! I love you so much!"

Dropping the grocery bags, Gail closed her eyes and embraced the girl's precious, warm weight. Inhaling the soft, sweet scent of her daughter's hair, she murmured, "Me, too, Lily. Me, too."

The double barn doors were open, ostensibly to let in light from the glow of the early-morning sun, but primarily so Samuel could hear the sound of a truck and trailer pulling up the lane. He pitchforked a flake of hay in front of their cow, Gabby. He'd been thinking about his driver since she'd dropped him off three days ago with barely a wave in his direction. His trip today might have more to do with the ride to and from the track than the Standardbreds there. But he wasn't going to tell his *bruder* that.

"I ran into Elam at the hardware store yesterday." Gideon's muffled voice came from the far side of Gabby, where he leaned his head against her flank as he milked the fawn-and-white cow.

Samuel stabbed the pitchfork into a nearby bale of alfalfa. He'd made time to see Elam the day before to ask his opinion on the trainers at the track. "He told me he's not regretting his decision to quit the business. Hope it wasn't just to make me feel good in taking it over. Seems hard to believe, but I look forward to today with even more excitement than I felt on my first one."

"*Ja.* Really hard to believe." The hiss of milk pinging against the metal sides of the pail punctuated his *bruder*'s words. "When were you going to tell me that the driver, Gail, was a woman? And a *yung* one at that?" Although his hands never stopped their steady rhythm, Gideon leaned back and shot his brother a glance. "Is that why you've been working like a madman the past few days? So you could fit in another trip to the track this week? I half expected the barn to be re-painted when I arrived home yesterday, the way you've rushed to get work done."

Samuel couldn't deny the accusation, as it was the truth. "The past few days were clear and the low humidity was good for cutting and drying the hay at our farm while it was down. I've got to get to Malachi's fields after that. And with the long evenings, there was plenty of light left after you got home yesterday to help me put up the bales. Just because I'm doing the majority of work on the farm doesn't mean that you can't occasionally get your hands dirty with it anymore."

"*Ach.* That's not what I mean, and my hands feel pretty full of farmwork right now." After a few final squirts, Gideon grabbed the handle of the bucket and stood from the three-legged milking stool where he'd been perched. "And after talking with Elam, I just wanted to know what I'm working for."

Samuel took the pail from him and poured its contents through a strainer into a metal milk can. "You're working for the farm." He set the pail down and shot his brother a grin. "And maybe a bit for your *bruder* to see a pretty girl again this week."

Gideon didn't share his smile. "As long as my *bruder* remembers that the pretty girl is *Englisch*."

Samuel's smile slipped. "Your *bruder* is very aware of that fact and doesn't need to be reminded." He stepped away to disinfect Gabby's udder and release her head from the wooden stanchion. The Guernsey stayed put, munching on the hay. "We met *Englisch* girls at *rumspringa* parties in Ohio before we moved. She's not the first girl who wasn't Amish who I've flirted with. Though I may stretch them at times, I know where the boundaries are." He placed a hand on Gabby's bony hip and met his brother's eyes. "When the time comes, I'll be baptized. I'm not leaving the Amish faith."

His younger brother's shoulders visibly relaxed and his mouth tipped up at the corners. "That's a relief. I thought so, but after watching the spring in your step even after the past few long days and finding out that the driver was a *yung* woman…and pretty—" his smile expanded "—your word, not Elam's, I was a little concerned over the glint in your eye when you spoke of your new business."

"*Mamm* will be glad you're here to take her place as mother hen. Malachi hasn't even been married a year yet and you're trying to get me married off, too? I said, when the time comes I'll be baptized into the church. Then I'll be married. But the time hasn't come, *bruder.* I'm not ready to settle down yet with *Gott*'s chosen one for me. This girl—" Samuel didn't know how to describe Gail, or his unaccustomed feeling for her "—is a challenge, that's all. Can you believe that she might not like your charming *bruder*?"

"It makes me think she has good sense."

Patting his brother on the shoulder, Samuel stepped back to pick up the milking stool and hang it on pegs on the barn's wall. His ears had picked up the sound of a vehicle approaching in the quiet morning. "No worries, then. Who wants to marry a sensible woman? Isn't Ruth enough to scare us off from that?" He winked at his brother, knowing that Gideon cared for his sister-in-law as much as he did.

His attention already on the approaching truck, he absently instructed, "Take some milk in for Ruth and Malachi and drop the rest off at the cheese factory."

"Like I do every day?"

He waved away Gideon's response, which

followed him out the barn's double doors, and watched Gail's truck and trailer pull into the lane. Maybe he was more than a little eager to see how long it would take him to get past this woman's defenses.

He'd sold the gelding. Made a slim profit, but a profit nonetheless. Although the Amish seemed a patriarchal society, the adage "happy wife, happy life" still applied. The wife had been happy with her new transportation, happy enough the husband had talked about it with some friends, drumming up a few more potential customers for Samuel.

The truck pulled into the lane and swung around in the farmyard. A moment later Samuel was sitting next to Gail in the worn cloth seat. He was immediately wary when she shot him a hooded look. He was used to women watching him closely, but not like they were just waiting for him to put a foot wrong. He hadn't been the recipient of a look like that since his *mamm* had to run an errand, leaving him alone in the kitchen with the cookies she'd just finished baking for a Christmas exchange.

"What?"

Gail didn't reply, just shifted the vehicle into Drive and the rig rattled down the lane.

That was when he realized they weren't alone.

Chapter Five

Samuel didn't know what prompted him to twist around to look in the backseat of the truck's cab. If it'd been a noise, it'd been a quiet one. But having turned, he stared for a moment. When he faced the front again, even though her eyes were on the road, he knew Gail was conscious of every breath he was taking. She was like a baseball batter in the box, braced for whatever he might pitch at her.

He casually leaned back into his seat. "Your sister?"

"My daughter." Eyes trained on the windshield, Gail's delicate jaw was shot forward, daring him to make a retort. And when he made one, it would be like shaking a wasp nest out of a tree. Although sometimes Samuel liked to poke at wasp nests, he knew this wasn't the day or the time.

Keeping his face neutral, he twisted around to take another look at the sleeping child.

"She's a beauty." And she was. Blonde where her mother was brunette, the little girl made a dainty portrait in her pink shirt, blue shorts and white tennis shoes. Her little rose-bud mouth was relaxed in sleep. The dark fan of her long eyelashes rested on porcelain cheeks.

Samuel faced the windshield again. "How old?"

"Three and a half." Gail's response was succinct but her graceful fingers relaxed their strangle of the steering wheel. From his angle, he had a clear view of them. No rings. Something he'd checked on day one. Amish women never wore jewelry, but *Englisch* women did. It still didn't mean anything, as some folks who did physical work didn't wear rings, either to protect the jewelry or to retain their fingers.

Samuel was surprised at the sudden sick feeling in his stomach at the thought that Gail's ring, one that proclaimed she belonged to another, might currently be in some esteemed place, waiting for her to come home and put it on. Surely it wasn't disappointment that was hollowing out his middle? There were always available girls out there; why would he feel so disappointed that Gail wasn't one of them?

Besides, she was *Englisch*. Samuel didn't know what his short-term future held in regard to women, but he knew his long-term one included baptism and raising a family in the Amish community.

His fingers drummed on the leg of his blue pants. After a few moments of silence, he could contain the question no longer. "Does your husband work in the horse business, too?"

"There is no husband, and her father's not in the picture." This time Gail did look at him. The intensity in her eyes reminded him of a doe with a fawn he'd accidentally cornered once in a field—defensive, wary, protective. He'd backed away then, giving them space to work their way out, escape to where the doe felt safe and secure. He did the same now. But for some reason, her statement made the day a little brighter, like the sun peeping back out after a threatening thundercloud.

Although he didn't see single, unmarried parenthood much in the Amish community, he knew it was there, although generally frowned upon. He also knew there were sometimes wedding dates moved up from the traditional late-fall wedding season because a *boppeli* was on the way. He didn't know how the Amish community in Miller's Creek handled those situations.

Amish or *Englisch*, it wasn't for him to judge. That was made clear in the *Biewel*.

"She like horses like her *mamm*?"

Gail's eyes flicked to the rearview mirror as she glanced at the sleeping girl. The hint of a smile touched her lips, and her shoulders eased back into the seat. "Loves them. Hard to keep her from walking right up to an unknown horse." She sighed. "I don't usually bring her to the track on workdays, but her babysitter was sick this morning and I had some jobs today that I couldn't afford to lose…"

While he was sympathetic to her situation, Samuel couldn't help but think that would never happen in the Amish community. Family was everything. There were always grandparents, older siblings, aunts or cousins on either side to help care for the *kinder*. The Plain life was wonderfully supportive. Being a young mother alone with a *kind* would be incredibly difficult. The prickly nature of his companion was becoming understandable, much like the doe at the fence.

Gail glanced in the rearview again. "Usually she drifts off after riding in the truck for a while. Hopefully, today will be one of those days. Otherwise—" she shook her head "—she can be a handful."

It was his turn to look in the rearview. The tiny girl didn't look like a handful. She looked sweet. Innocent. Samuel generally got along with women of all ages. He wanted the one sharing the front seat of the truck to like him. Maybe assisting with the one in the back would help.

"If she decides that today is not one for resting, she can stay with me."

Gail looked at him as if one of her equine passengers had spoken to her. "You're kidding."

Samuel was mildly insulted. "Why would I be kidding? I have several younger siblings, I've been around *kinder* before. My *bruder* Malachi is going to be a father. Maybe I want to practice at being an *onkel*?"

She snorted. "They don't start out this size. Let me tell you, there's a big difference between a *boppeli* and a three-year-old."

"But they do get there. And to me, they're less scary at this size." He cradled an arm like he was holding an infant. "That initial small bundle is more frightening than anything. I'd rather handle a fractious thousand pound Standardbred. Your daughter, I won't be afraid to drop."

Gail shot him a skeptical glance.

"Not that I would, but at least she isn't as helpless."

"No, she isn't that." Her lips curved into a rueful smile. "It's when she's insistent on being helpful that problems usually arise."

They rode in silence until they reached the outer edge of Milwaukee. If Gail's bouncing left leg and gnawed bottom lip were any indications, she was deep in thought about his offer. "If you're sure?"

"I'm always sure."

She snorted in response. "If you have any trouble, most of the folks in George's stable block know her. They're too busy to keep her for long, but someone there might be able to give you a break."

"I'm sure we'll be fine."

They pulled into the track's back parking lot. "I have a couple of local hauls." Gail checked the rearview mirror. Samuel didn't turn, but the little girl must still be sleeping, as she continued, "Hopefully, she'll be good through those. I'll look for you when I get back."

Samuel nodded. "I'm serious about my offer."

He pulled the door handle and started to

slip out of the cab when a sleepy little voice murmured from the back. "Who are you?"

Standing at the open door of the still-running truck, he looked across the front seat at Gail. Hand poised over the gearshift, her blue eyes were round with apprehension.

Samuel heard the childish voice again, a little less sleepy, a little more indignant. "Mommy. I want out."

"Hey, sweetie. Mommy needs to drive for a bit. I've got an appointment. We'll get out later." Gail left the truck in Park and turned toward the backseat.

"I want out *now*."

Through the back window of the truck, Samuel could see miniature legs kicking against the seat, the action coordinating with the thumping he could hear from inside the cab. He had to smile. The daughter was as direct as her mother.

"We'll just ride for a bit longer, then we'll get out."

"Been riding. I want *out*." The little girl bent her head, and her hands went to the buckle at the center of a number of straps on her car seat. Samuel raised his eyebrows when, after fiddling a moment with the buckle, the straps came loose. A second later she was wiggling out of the seat.

"Lily! We talked about not getting out until Mommy said it was okay. You need to get back into your seat, young lady." Looking at Samuel, Gail shook her head in bewilderment. "I don't know how she does that."

"Please say it's okay to get out, Mommy, please?"

Samuel didn't know about Gail, or being a *mamm*, but he melted at the pleading in the child's voice.

Apparently, her *mamm* wasn't unaffected, either. Gail looked to where Samuel silently stood at the door. "I got her up so early after the sitter let me know she was sick and couldn't watch her today. As we're in the same building, usually Lily stays in bed until she wakes up. I guess I can't blame her for wanting out now." Gail's features went from a guilty uncertainty to piercing him with an accusatory gaze like he'd disagreed with her. "She's not spoiled. I try not to spoil her. She's usually a pretty happy girl."

At the swirling emotions, Samuel felt a moment of gratitude that in an Amish community the women raised the *kinder* and the men raised the barns. You might bang your head barn building, but it probably wouldn't impact your mental state as much as child-raising seemed to. He hadn't spent that much time with his younger siblings during the day when they were little; he'd already had responsibilities working outside. If this was the way it felt to care for a child, he was rethinking his suggestion. But it was too late; he'd made it.

"My offer still stands."

Gail looked torn. "She won't stay in her car seat and I'll be at places where I don't know the horses or the people. If she gets out when I'm not looking…" She inhaled raggedly.

A pint-sized hand reached through the space between the seats and rested on Gail's arm. "Please let me out, Mommy. I'm hungry."

Gail closed her eyes and seemed to come to a decision. When she opened them and pinned him with a look, Samuel knew the decision included him. "Lily, I'd like you to meet Samuel."

Leaning back into the cab, Samuel came face-to-face with the wide-awake Lily, who'd poked her head over the folded armrest into the front seat. Her bright blue eyes solemnly took him in. "Why does he wear a hat? Can I wear a hat?"

"You have a hat in your backpack." Gail reached between the seats to pull out a dainty purple pack from the floor and set it on the passenger seat. It was a small version of what Samuel had seen *Englisch* schoolchildren wear. "There's a banana and some peanut butter crackers in there, as well as a juice carton. That should hold her until I get back for lunch." Gone was the indecisive mother. Now that a decision had been made, she was all business. "You do have a cell phone, don't you? Your bishop lets you carry a phone for your job? Elam did. Of course you do. You've contacted me on it. Give it here." She reached out her hand.

"Uh, yes." Actually, like many men in their *rumspringa*, he'd carried a phone before he'd undertaken the job. He just wasn't used to a woman demanding it. Samuel fished it out and handed it to her. Without a word, her fingers worked rapidly over the screen before she handed it back.

"Okay. I just sent a text to myself so I'm the first message up. Call me if you need anything. I also put in George's phone number. He's well acquainted with Lily. Depending on what he's doing, he might be able to get to you faster." She frowned. "Maybe I should just call him and see what he's got going on today."

Samuel was a bit stung that she didn't think

he was capable. "I can do it." He turned his attention to Lily. "We'll get along just fine."

Two matching sets of big blue eyes regarded him skeptically.

"I want out."

"There's also an extra set of clothes in there, in case of an accident, or she gets into something. And a little coloring book and crayons. She'll tell you if she has to go potty. Most of the female grooms know her and can help."

Samuel's eyes widened. Maybe he should have kept his mouth shut. He was trying to build a business here, and Elam had said that required building trust. How much trust could he build while stopping a potential transaction to arrange a bathroom trip for a little one? But he'd offered, and in his business and life, a man was only as good as his word. He cleared his throat. "Okay. Anything else?"

Gail's forehead wrinkled for a moment. "No, she's pretty good about communicating what she needs." For the first time that morning, a real smile crossed her face. "Be prepared for questions." She reached out her hands to her daughter, who scrambled through the opening over the armrest into the front seat. "Lily, you're going to spend the morning with Samuel. He likes horses, too. In fact, last week I took a nice gelding to his place. Maybe he'll tell you about him."

She reached out her hand and Samuel found himself holding the purple backpack. "I'll call or text you later to check on her." Gail glanced at her watch. Her eyes, looking from her daughter to Samuel, held uncertainty and guilt. "I have to go."

Samuel opened his arms and, at her mother's encouragement, the girl went warily into them. He ducked back out of the cab, shut the door and stepped away from the truck. Gail pierced him with a stare through the open truck window. Samuel almost took a step back. If he'd have been a lesser man, he would've wilted under the intensity of her blue gaze.

"I'm trusting you because I don't have a lot of choice and Elam trusted you. And for all I've seen, you're a good guy. But if anything happens to my daughter..." Her tone and narrowed eyes left no guesstimate necessary on his condition should Lily not be hale and hearty at the end of the day. Samuel grinned. He'd experienced half-ton cows charging him when he was trying to take care of their calves that were less intimidating.

Bouncing the little girl in his arms, who was regarding him as suspiciously as her *mamm*, he assured them both, "We'll be fine. It'll be an adventure for both of us."

Gail turned her attention to her daughter. "Bye, sweetie. I'll see you later. Love you. Be good for Samuel." She put the truck in gear, and it and the trailer rolled away, leaving Samuel and his small charge looking after it.

If he was such a good guy, why had there been tears sparkling in the backs of her eyes? Samuel turned to look at the pint-sized passenger in his arms. She reached out and poked the brim of his straw hat with a tiny finger, pushing it back on his head.

"Can I wear a hat, too?"

Samuel took a deep breath as he met Lily's blue eyes. His whole day would be based on how he handled the next few moments. *Ach*, the first thing he'd learned about women was to start with a smile. The second, somehow you needed to give them what they wanted or at least make them think you would. Shifting the little blonde in his arms, he pulled up the backpack so he could unzip it. "Let's check in here. Your *mamm* said you had a hat. She's been right about many things so she's probably right about this, as well."

He rummaged past a banana, some other snacks and a few bright-colored clothes to find a petite purple baseball cap. "Is this it?" Triumphantly, he pulled it from the pack.

"I want a hat like yours."

"Well, one would be difficult to find here today. But if we get along well, later I'll let you wear mine for a while."

She considered the bargain for a moment. "Okay."

He slipped the purple hat on her head and, one-handed, worked the little ponytail through the back. Now what? Fishing out the banana, he offered it to her. "Are you hungry? Your *mamm* said you were up early."

"She's not my *mamm*, she's my mommy."

"*Ach*, you're right. *Mamm* is the word I grew up using for *mother*."

"Why didn't you use *mommy*?"

Samuel sighed as he looked into her curious eyes and thought wistfully about barn-raising. "Would you like to see some horses?"

Lily smiled. "I like horses."

Slinging the pack over his shoulder, he shifted her onto his hip and started for the entrance to the stable block. "Let's go see them, then. Let's see lots and lots of horses."

By the time they reached the main avenue, Samuel understood Gail's warning regarding questions. After a short hike, when he was carrying her again—too much human and equine traffic for her to be down on the ground—Lily tugged on the black suspenders that ran across the tops of his shoulders.

"What are these?"

"They're suspenders."

"Why do you wear them?"

Samuel blinked. He'd never imagined talking with a girl about clothing articles. Lily stared at him from her perch in his arms, waiting for an answer. "They keep my pants from falling down."

Her rosebud lips frowned. "My mommy doesn't wear them and her pants don't fall down."

Ach. "They're for men." It seemed like a pretty good response, until Lily began twisting her head this way and that. He smiled as her soft ponytail repeatedly brushed his cheek.

"He doesn't have them. And he doesn't have them. And they're boys." Lily pointed to men working nearby as they walked from the stables to the track. She looked up at Samuel, as if daring him to refute her observation.

"You're right, Lily. I wear them because I'm Amish."

Her brow furrowed. "What's an A… Amiss?"

Ach. "Well, Amish people are people who choose to live a certain way." Samuel suppressed a smile. The next question would be how and why people choose to live differently than others. Samuel didn't think he had the capability of explaining that to a three-year-old.

He slipped the purple cap off her head and replaced it with his own straw one. Lily's head disappeared underneath it. "How about you wear my hat for a while?" His distraction proved a success when she tipped it back and gave him a toothy grin. It expanded when he set the purple cap on his head. "We'll switch." At Lily's giggle, Samuel thought he might have the knack for *kinder* care as well as barn building.

A while later they'd worked their way to the rail along the track, where he wanted to watch the horses run time trials. Gail had already texted to check on them. Twice. Samuel assured her they were fine. Lily was fed, content wearing her own hat and seemed intrigued enough with the current surroundings that a few moments were free of question asking.

Samuel watched the trio of horses coming around the curve of the track, their gleaming brown coats in contrast to the white rail behind them. One was falling behind as they came down the stretch. Cocking his head,

Samuel focused on the mutterings of the trainer leaning on the fence a few yards away. A pearl of wisdom from Elam, the previous Amish trader, was the more the trainer complained about a horse, the cheaper the price. Based on the man's conversation to his companion, this one might go pretty cheap indeed.

A few minutes earlier Lily had insisted on being set down. She'd been busy in the powdery dirt by the fence, making little piles and then tramping on them with her miniature sneakers. Puffs of dust had drifted up with each stomp to coat her bare legs. Samuel hoped the rules of the day hadn't included keeping the little girl clean. If so, he was a failure at *kinder* minding.

"Well, Lily. Think we ought to inquire about that gelding?" He glanced down to where she'd been playing at his feet.

There was no purple ball cap over a blond ponytail between him and the fence. Samuel peered up and down the fence row before spinning to look behind him. "Lily?"

Chapter Six

Samuel frantically scanned the corridor between the rail and the stands. People passed by alone and in groups but everyone was hip high or taller. Spying a flash of purple, Samuel dodged around a pair of trainers only to discover the bright color had been the silks of a passing driver. Swiveling his head, Samuel searched the surrounding area. "Lily!"

Where could she have gone? She was there a moment ago. Samuel's heart pounded so hard he felt the accelerated beat in his ears. "Lily!" Grabbing the rail, he vaulted into the stands and ran up several rows of empty bleacher seats to get a better view. A group of eight trotters took the track and were warming up before their time trials. Samuel caught his breath at their churning legs. What if Lily wandered onto the track in front of the racing horses? He scoured the track, the infield and the surrounding perimeter. Nothing.

Cupping his hands around his mouth like he would when calling cows at the farm, Samuel hollered as loud as he could, "Lily!" People stopped and looked at him askance, but he didn't care. What should he do? He didn't even know her last name. Not seeing Lily's diminutive form from his current position, Samuel raced up to the top row of the stadium, chastising himself with every lunging stride for being more interested in flirting with her mother than learning about his small charge. *Please,* Gott, *help me find her. Help her to be all right.*

When he reached the top railing, he gripped it with white knuckles and looked out toward the stable block and parking lot. The panorama before him laid out the racetrack in miniature.

How could he find her? How could he not?

A cold sweat trickled down the indentation of his spine as he scrutinized the area below for a little girl in a pink shirt and purple hat. Nothing. Nothing. But…wait! A small figure was threading its way through the horse and human traffic between the track and the stables. A few folks turned to watch as it flitted by. Could it be? *Please,* Gott*!* Samuel cupped his hands around his mouth again.

"Lily!"

The figure paused and spun around.

"Lily! Stay right there!"

Faces were upturned in his direction. Samuel pointed to Lily and called again, "Lily, stay right there!" He held his breath until a passing groom, leading a Standardbred from the horse walker, directed the bay over to the girl and said something to her. They both looked up toward Samuel. He waved frantically and they both waved back.

Whirling, Samuel sprinted down the steps of the bleachers three at a time, his work boots clanking on the aluminum planks. He wove his way through the human and equine crowd at a jog and finally reached the waiting groom and little girl. Swinging Lily into his arms, Samuel was so thrilled to find her the words that spilled out were the first language he'd learned and not English. The groom regarded him curiously.

"*Denki, denki.* I can't thank you enough."

The groom nodded and moved on with his charge.

"*Ach*, Lily, I couldn't find you. I was afraid I lost you."

"I was right here." Lily frowned at him.

"*Ja*, that might be so, but I didn't know that. Why did you leave? Where were you going?"

"You said we could get a hot dog when we got hungry." She pointed toward the snack shack they'd passed earlier that morning. "I was hungry so I was getting a hot dog."

"Ah…" She had him there. "When I said that, I meant we'd go together."

"You were busy."

With his heart still pounding at his scare and relief in having found her, Samuel didn't feel capable of reasoning with a three-year-old. He inhaled his first full breath since he'd looked down to find her missing. It shuddered out of him, taking the tension with it. "Let's go get one now." So what if it was before ten o'clock in the morning.

Moments later, hot dogs in hand, they wandered to George Hayes's section of the stables. They found the trainer by one of his stall doors, frowning at the occupant inside. At Lily's enthusiastic greeting, he turned as they approached.

"Well, hello there, Lily. How are you?"

"We're eating because Samuel lost me."

Samuel winced as the blonde passenger in his arms patted his shoulder.

George eyed him closely. "He did, did he? Looks like he found you again."

"Yup, he didn't lose me for long," Lily acknowledged before finishing her last bite of hot dog.

Flushing, Samuel finished his own before responding, "*Ach*, there's not many secrets, is there? She was hungry. I'm hoping eating at this hour doesn't break any rules."

The trainer smiled. "No, no secrets at that age. You might want to tell Gail your version first, before someone else—" he tipped his head at Lily "—reports it. It'll be all right. She's pretty forgiving."

Samuel blinked at the surprising assessment of the intense woman he was getting to know. "Maybe on food. But probably not if I lost her daughter."

"Well, you're right about that. She'd do about anything for her little girl." The man's eyebrow was raised, probably wondering what Samuel, apparently an incompetent *kinder* minder, was doing with Lily.

Aware of the poor impression he might be giving this friend of Gail's, Samuel hastened to explain, "Her sitter was sick. She was in a bind."

George nodded. "Single parenting is tough. I don't know how she does it."

After spending part of the morning with her daughter, neither did Samuel.

Conversation stopped when a horse stuck its head over the stable's half door. Eyes ringed with white, it snorted at them and disappeared back into the stall.

George leaned on the stall's half door. "Got a bit of a bind myself. An owner wants to reduce his animals by one. I'm trying to determine which one goes. This filly's got promise, but she might need too much work to get it realized."

Securing Lily on his hip, Samuel stepped closer and looked over the door, as well. A bay filly stood at the back of the stall, head high, watching them warily. Her beautiful lines and attitude reminded him of his mare, Belle, who was also nervous, flashy and not for everyone. But for a few adventurous young men in their *rumspringa*, the filly would be a perfect fit.

"I must be quite the problem solver today, because I think I can help you out with your situation, as well."

Having someone fall asleep against his shoulder was a unique sensation. The afternoon sun and busy day had tired Lily out. Her hat was off and stowed in the backpack. Some of her blond bangs were clumped together, slightly sweaty from the warm day. Samuel tried to imagine the level of trust it took to let someone relax like that. He'd had girls lay their heads on his shoulder on rides home after Sunday night singings, but those situations had been edged with conscious ardor instead of sincere trust.

Lily hadn't been out for long. The steady rhythm of her breathing, the miniature hand curled under his chin, shifted something in Samuel. The urge to guard her sleep like a Great Pyrenees dog protected its sheep was overwhelming.

It'd been a great day in spite of, or maybe because of, his pint-sized companion. Gail had called several times to ensure they were doing all right. She called at noon, her distress evident through the phone, explaining another job opportunity had come up for the day, but she wouldn't take it if there was any problem whatsoever with Lily. Samuel assured her they were fine. And they were, now that he always kept one eye on the little girl no matter what they were doing. In the early afternoon, Gail texted him to meet her by George's stable block. He and Lily found a bench in the shade and sat down to wait.

He'd managed to buy two horses during the day, the gelding that'd been slow down the final stretch and George's filly. Samuel didn't figure to keep the fretful horse long, but expected she'd be a nuisance while he did.

Seeing Gail stride into view with another trainer down the stable row, Samuel carefully shifted his sleeping burden and stood. By the time he quietly approached, Gail was bent at a makeshift table outside the stalls, flipping through some paperwork. Coming up on her right side, he saw her scrawl her signature at the bottom of a page.

Curious as to her full name, since she hadn't yet mentioned it, Samuel tilted his head to read the paper. He froze at the sight of it.

Abigail Lapp.

He darted an assessing glance at the po-nytailed, jean-clad woman beside him as a number of curious things now made sense.

As the Amish culture had begun with a limited number of families and for all practical purposes remained a closed society, there were still a limited number of surnames across the communities. Some were more prevalent than others.

Lapp was one of the most common.

Of course, *Lapp* could be a surname in the *Englisch* world, as well. But Samuel recalled how easily she'd spoken and pronounced Amish words. He'd thought at the time it was because of her hours riding with Elam. Now he wondered.

And there was her abruptly changed behavior when they'd met Ruth and Hannah... Hannah *Lapp*, coming down his lane. And he wondered some more.

The *Englisch* would be surprised how many Amish youth chose to stay in their community at the end of their *rumspringa*. A small percentage, though, for various reasons, did leave. The woman beside him was apparently one of them. And Samuel figured the little girl in his arms was at least part of the reason.

Gail flipped the sheets back down after confirming the delivery. Aware that someone had approached, she looked over as she straightened from the table. Her breath caught at the sight of her sleeping daughter in Samuel's strong arms. A bolt of longing for that kind of security shot through her. She reached for her daughter.

"How was she? I can't thank you enough for watching her today. I feel so terrible leaving her with you but she would've been miserable with me all day."

"I've got her if you don't want to risk waking her in the exchange." Samuel kept his arm under the little girl. "And don't scold yourself. It must be difficult to raise a *kind* alone, unlike in the Amish community, where there's always help around."

Gail's gaze flew to Samuel's blue eyes as she dropped her arms. Surely he didn't know? No secret could be kept with Lily around, but she'd never talked with her daughter about her past. Lily wouldn't have known any secrets to spill. Gail smiled weakly.

"She hasn't been out that long. She must've run out of questions." Samuel's lips curved. "For the moment."

Gail winced. "Was she a handful?"

"*Ach*, we got along. She probably now knows more about the Plain people than most of my *Englisch* neighbors."

Was there an emphasis on some of his words? Tensing again, Gail searched Samuel's eyes. They revealed nothing.

"I bought a couple of horses today. When do you want to load them?"

Grateful for the change of topic, Gail nodded. "I'm ready to go now, if you are."

Casting another glance at her sleeping daughter, she fell in step beside Samuel as they traveled down the shed row to collect his purchases. She took control of the horses while Samuel continued to carry Lily to the truck. When they reached the rig, they switched; Samuel loaded the Standardbreds without incident while Gail fastened her still-sleeping daughter into the car seat.

When Samuel was quiet all the way out of town, Gail covertly glanced at her passenger. He was looking out the window, seemingly deep in thought. Sighing, she left him to them. She'd almost hyperventilated this morning about leaving Lily with him at the track. Sanity had kicked in again but she'd worried all day that she'd done the right thing,

He wasn't a stranger. He had several references. Elam, who was as honest as they came, had spoken highly of Samuel. Ruth Fisher, whom Gail respected, had married his brother, so she must've thought the family was all right. And Hannah, her own sister, who was as sweet and perfect as they came, apparently associated with him. The man couldn't drive and didn't have a vehicle, so it wasn't as if he was going to abscond with her daughter.

Besides, Gail knew about everyone at the track and many knew Lily, so they'd had support on hand.

It would've been a miserable time for Lily, cooped up all day in the truck. And losing this day's business and related prospects would've put Gail much closer to losing the rig and their livelihood.

Gail sneaked another glance at Samuel. Yes, she'd made the right decision. She just needed to stop wishing she could've spent the day with them, as well.

They rode in comfortable silence except for the wind blowing in the open window, until they almost reached his farm. Not knowing when she'd see him again, Gail was surprisingly reluctant to completely let the afternoon go without talking to him.

"I like the gelding. What made you buy the skittish filly?"

She felt his gaze on her as she slowed to turn into his lane. "I've got someone in mind for her. Benjamin Raber admired my mare, Belle, when he and I worked together at my *bruder*'s furniture business. I thought he'd like a similar sort. If not him, there are plenty of young men in their *rumspringa* who wouldn't mind a flashy ride."

Gail remembered Benjamin Raber. Years ago, if she'd walked out with the quiet, dark-haired man, instead of being bedazzled by the blond, charismatic Atlee, she wouldn't have left the Amish community. Her lips twisted for what might have been. But then she wouldn't have had Lily. She couldn't imagine life without her daughter.

As they drove up the lane, a young Amish man, most likely Samuel's brother from the similar build and blond hair, stepped out of the barn. Gail circled the yard and backed the trailer toward the big double doors. Samuel got out. Glancing toward the backseat, he carefully swung the passenger door in, leaving it open a crack.

Upon rolling the windows the rest of the way down and shutting off the truck, Gail twisted in her seat to check on Lily. Head propped against the side of the car seat, mouth slightly open, her daughter was still sleeping hard. It must've been a big day. Surely she'd sleep for the short time it'd take to unload the horses before they were back on the road. Gail smiled before glancing at her watch. Lily would be raring to go when she woke up. And talkative. If her mother asked a few probing questions about her daughter's day with her handsome companion, well, it would be perfectly understandable.

With one last look at Lily, Gail slid from the truck and closed the door with a quiet click.

Samuel was releasing the latch on the back of the trailer when Gail rounded its corner.

Seeing her flick a glance toward Gideon, he nodded toward his brother. "Gail, my *bruder* Gideon. He's not always sitting around the barn waiting for company. Sometimes he's actually in town working."

"I'm working whether I'm in town or home. Which I wouldn't have to do if you'd just get things done a little faster around here," retorted Gideon as he pushed the double barn doors behind them farther open.

"I'd have more time outside to get things done if I didn't have to do most of the cooking. I can't even get the hogs to eat what you make for supper."

Gail's lips twitched at their good-natured bickering. She nodded at Gideon and stepped out of the way as Samuel opened the door at the back of the trailer and swung it with a squeal of stubborn hinges to the right. The thud of hooves against metal rang as the two horses inside shifted at the activity. Not surprisingly, most of the thuds came from the fractious filly fastened nearest the trailer's front.

Samuel stepped inside and untied the gelding, who, although head up and ears twitching, backed smoothly out. Giving the bay a soothing pat as the horse took in his new surroundings, Samuel wheeled him around and led him toward the double doors, where he handed the lead over to his brother.

"Would you take him on in, Gideon? The filly's like a twin sister to Belle and probably won't come out of the trailer so calmly."

Gideon ran a hand down the gelding's neck. "Don't know why you're attracted to that type."

"Probably because they're fast and flashy and I get requests for them. In fact, I may let you have a chance at this one before I tell Benjamin about her." Gideon snorted and headed through the barn doors with the gelding. Samuel turned back toward the trailer. Gail was already inside, untying the filly's lead. "*Ach*, I'll get her out," he called, striding back to help.

"I got her." Gail finished untying the lead and eased the excited filly from the mobile stall. Stepping to the right, out of the way of the pair, Samuel watched warily as the bay kept throwing her head as Gail gently and competently backed her from the trailer.

He knew the Standardbred had been transported many times, but one wouldn't know it to watch her antics. The other horses in the barn and pasture called out greetings to the newcomer, adding to the filly's agitation.

Once they were on the ground, Gail turned

the sweating filly toward the large barn doors. With a loud creak, the trailer door started to swing shut, just as Gideon emerged through the double doors from the shadow of the barn's interior.

It was too much for the horse. She reared, almost lifting Gail from the ground.

As Samuel lunged toward them, he saw a flash of pink beyond the swinging trailer door. To his horror, he realized Lily had gotten out of the truck and was approaching them.

Without hesitation, he whipped around the swaying door and swept Lily into his arms. A loud clang of hooves striking metal rang in his ears an instant before the door slammed into his back, a sharp edge plowing into his shoulder.

The blow jolted him forward. He heard Gail's sharp cry behind him as, clutching Lily to his chest, he staggered toward the ground.

Chapter Seven

Samuel went down hard on one knee.

Seconds later Gail was at his side. "Are you okay?"

Eyes closed, teeth gritted, Samuel breathed through the explosion in his shoulder blade a moment before he could speak. "Check Lily. If she's all right, we're all right." Easing down to both knees, he loosened his arms from the rigid grip he had on the little girl.

His anxious gaze matched Gail's as they searched Lily's pale face. The child turned her wide eyes to Samuel before breaking into a toothy grin. "Do it again!"

Samuel winced as he exhaled sharply. "I think not." Carefully releasing her, he ensured she was on her feet before dropping his arms. Gail immediately snatched her daughter into a tight hug. Shifting back onto his heels, Samuel pushed slowly to his feet. Once there, he rested a hand against the trailer as he dropped his head and panted in time with the throb in his back.

Gail looked up from where she held her daughter, gratitude evident in her blue eyes.

"Mommy, you're hugging me too tight." Lily wiggled free of Gail's embrace.

Samuel sent a prayer of thanks to *Gott* for the little girl's safety. Feeling a light touch on his shoulder, he turned to Gideon.

"Your shirt is ripped and bloody." Concern was etched on his *bruder*'s face. They worked enough around livestock and farming to know injuries could be frequent and debilitating. "Better see if you can get Ruth to wash it out for you, as I'm not going to try."

Samuel forced his wince into a smile. "You'd do a poor job of it anyway. Where's the filly?"

"I put her in one of the open stalls." At Samuel's relieved nod, he continued, "I think I'll pass. Give Benjamin a chance on her. You don't seem to be enough judge of horseflesh to bring one home yet that I'd be interested in." Gideon mirrored Samuel's false smile, but his eyes asked how bad it was.

Shifting away from the trailer, Samuel

hissed in a breath as he straightened his back. "Sore, yes. Broken, no."

"Gut." Gideon's tense shoulders eased under his suspenders. "Then I won't have to take off work to help you finish the haying at Malachi's."

"I want to take a look at your shoulder." Gail joined them, an interested Lily by her side.

"Ach, it's not the first bruise I've gotten from a horse. It won't be the last."

"That may be, but it's the first one you've gotten while protecting my daughter. Let's go into the house. We're going to take a look at it." Gail tipped her head toward the white farmhouse, indicating that Samuel should lead the way.

Samuel and Gideon exchanged a look. Gideon smiled. "What is it about my *brieder* and bossy women?" He hooked a thumb toward the barn. "I'll get the new arrivals settled in. " Nodding to Gail and Lily, his smile expanded to a face-splitting grin. "Pleasure to meet you. I look forward to seeing you again sometime. Holler if he doesn't behave while you're patching him up. Try not to make him cry."

Samuel rolled his eyes. "Just go take care of my horses," he tossed over his shoulder as he started for the house. "I'll see if I can find a little pony in my travels and buy him for you to drive. Maybe that'd be something you could handle. In case you're worried, I'll have Lily here check it out to make sure the pony is safe enough for you."

"She'd be a better judge of horseflesh than you." Gideon's response followed them across the farmyard.

Samuel smiled, although it probably looked more like a grimace. His shoulder was on fire. While walking beside Gail toward the house, he slowed when he saw Lily dodge around her mother to come along his side. To his surprise, the girl reached for his hand. Her small one only wrapped around two of his fingers, but the feeling that rushed through him at the miniature grip almost made him stumble. She looked up at him, her blue eyes as concerned as his *bruder*'s had been.

"I'm sorry you have an owie."

Samuel touched her hair with his other hand. "It's all right, Lily. I'm just glad that you don't." He'd take his throbbing shoulder and more if it meant Gail and her daughter were safe.

Gail cleared her throat against the sudden lump that'd lodged there at the sight of her daughter walking hand in hand with Samuel. As Gail had no time and even less interest in men, it meant, other than George and some of the grooms at the track, Lily had no male figures in her life. To see her daughter connect so strongly and quickly with this particular one, who made her mother feel the same way… Pressing her lips together, Gail relived seeing the metal door hurling toward the pair. She forced back the tears of relief that they were all right. A glance at Samuel's bloody back amended that. Well, mostly all right.

Recalling the first time she laid eyes on him in this farmyard, Gail acknowledged maybe she'd misjudged the charming Amish man. Certainly, he was pretty on the outside, but there were depths that she hadn't anticipated.

Upon reaching the farmhouse, Gail looked through the screen door into its shadowed interior. Rooted on the porch, she took a few shallow breaths and cleared her throat again before she pulled the door open with a squeak. Heart hammering, Gail crossed the threshold.

It could've been her parents' kitchen. The gas-powered stove and refrigerator, a fireplace situated between the kitchen and living room, kerosene lamps and gaslights positioned at key locations. Pegs on the wall bordered the doors, ready for hats and coats. Even if the ample windows hadn't let in the late-afternoon light, Gail wouldn't have bothered looking for a light switch. She knew there wouldn't be one.

She also knew the plainness of the decor wasn't just because it was a bachelor household. Her family's home had been spartan, as well. The Schrock home had no decorations on the walls, no pictures; only a few wooden shelves held a lamp and a windup clock whose ticktock followed them as Samuel guided them through large, sparsely furnished rooms. Rooms big and open enough to be used for church services when it was the owner's turn to host.

The bare walls weren't lost on Lily. "Why don't you have any pictures? Do you need some pictures? I can make you some. I'm a good drawer. Mommy says so."

Samuel grinned down at her daughter. "Thank you. That would sure make a difference in here, wouldn't it?" He led them across a large living area to push open the door to a small, utilitarian bathroom.

Samuel turned on an overhead gaslight and they stepped in. There wasn't much space in the room for one, much less two. When Lily squeezed in as well, pressing Gail against Samuel's solid frame, she inhaled a startled breath of sun-warmed flesh and a whiff of horse. Unthinking, Gail put a hand on his upper arm to catch herself, before dropping it like she'd touched a burning coal when she felt the lean muscles tense under her fingers.

"Lily! What do you say?" Embarrassed, Gail shuffled back in the limited space and directed Samuel to sit on the edge of a simple white tub.

"Excuse me," Lily offered disinterestedly as she continued to explore.

Shifting out of the way so Samuel could remove his shirt, both he and Gail hissed in a breath when he managed to do so. Him, surely in pain; her, in sympathy of the angry wound.

Samuel regarded the torn and bloody garment remorsefully. "I'm running out of shirts."

Gail reached out a hand. Having been one of two older sisters with several young brothers in the house, cleaning and mending shirts was something she well remembered how to do. "I'll take it home and mend it."

She almost smiled at the hopeful look Samuel gave her as he handed it over. "I have some other shirts and socks that need some help, as well…?"

As a distraction, it helped. Anything to take her mind off the bare torso in front of her. "Can't coax your sister-in-law to take care of them for you?"

"*Ach, nee.* Ruth's too strong-minded to be coaxed into anything she doesn't want to do."

"Don't you have a sweetheart? Why haven't you married?" Gail could've bitten her tongue at the questions that popped out. The prospect gave her a pang. Amish courtships were generally kept secret until the couple's betrothal was announced at church. Her pang became a stab at the memory of how well she knew that fact.

What stung more now was the possibility that Samuel could be walking out with someone and she wouldn't know it. It wasn't as if she was attending Sunday night singings to witness if he was driving someone home afterward, but even that wasn't always a telltale sign.

Gail edged her way past a fascinated Lily to the simple sink. Using the soap there, she washed her hands before she rinsed the basin, set the plug and ran water into it, grateful that it was plumbed for hot water. A quick look around revealed a basket of well-worn washcloths on a shelf under the sink. "Do you have iodine? Or antiseptic ointment? The skin's broken. The handle must've hit you. The door on my trailer probably has enough germs on it that I'd feel better if we treated you with something."

Samuel grunted as she dabbed the gash on his shoulder with the soapy washcloth. "Check the shelf under the sink. There should be a first-aid kit somewhere close. We get poked or stepped on enough that we usually keep something around."

He stiffened as she gently probed the broken skin over his shoulder blade. Although bloody and angry-looking, to her relief, it didn't look like it would need stitches. But it was going to be sore.

"What's that? It looks like cheese." Lily squeezed her way to the sink and poked a square white block sitting on the back of it.

"That's soap, sweetie." Gail remembered making similar bars many times over.

"Why is it so white and square?"

"Because it's homemade."

"Like ice cream?"

"Kind of. Don't eat it, as it probably has lye in it." Gail glanced at Samuel for confirmation.

"*Ja.* My sister-in-law Ruth's efforts. She

was making all sorts of things when she first stopped working at the shop after she got married. The woman can't sit still." He touched Lily on the nose. "Like someone else I know."

Lily giggled before looking solemnly into Samuel's face. "Are you going to cry?"

"I'll try not to. But if I do, don't tell my *bruder*."

Gail appreciated her daughter's presence. If it'd been just the two of them, it would've felt too intimate in the small space, even with his injury. She was trying to be as gentle as she could with the wound, but under her touch, she could feel Samuel's occasional flinch.

He'd never responded to her wife question. Had that been accidental or intentional? Gail wondered how many old female friends and acquaintances had him in their dreams, if not in their sights. It brought back memories of excitement she'd felt when she'd entered her *rumspringa*. Of her pounding heart when handsome, charming Atlee started paying attention to her. She'd thought at first that his insistence on a secretive relationship was exciting. Now she knew why they'd had to sneak around. He'd convinced Louisa, who he'd been seeing first, of the same necessity. Stomach twisting, she recalled Atlee's betrayal and the fool she'd been. She dabbed at the back before her more fiercely. Samuel recoiled and slanted her a look. Instantly contrite, Gail gentled her touch.

Lily slipped out of the bathroom. Hands on nonexistent hips, she glanced around the living area of the house. "Where's your TV?"

Samuel's lips twitched. "Don't have one. They take electricity, which we also don't have."

"Huh." Lily took a few steps farther into the open area room. "Well, that's weird."

"Remember, we talked today about Amish choosing to live differently? That's one of the ways we live differently."

"How do you watch cartoons?"

"We don't. We do other things." Samuel's attention was focused on Lily, but his voice had gotten huskier as Gail administered to his back.

Gail was glad she didn't have to speak. She didn't know if she could've at the moment. Setting the washcloth on the edge of the sink, she washed and dried her hands again before rummaging on the shelf under it for the first-aid kit. Finding it, she extracted the antiseptic ointment and squeezed some on her fingertip.

Exhaling a stream of air through pursed lips, she stared down at the tanned, muscular back. As she touched the angry wound without the barrier of the washcloth, a flush crept up her cheeks. Gail trained her focus on her daughter's chatter.

Lily's words reminded Gail that her choices for her life would be Lily's life, as well. Much as she longed for home and Plain life, could she take her daughter from the world she'd grown up knowing? Lily didn't know the world Gail had grown up in. One of playing Scrabble or checkers with siblings instead of watching TV. Of hard work, but taking much joy in that work. Of community, of family unity, of visiting friends and frolics.

What was right for them both?

It wasn't the man whose back she ministered to. Gail cleared her throat twice before she could speak. "Um, there're some large bandages in the kit that I'll use to cover it to keep it clean. Then I think I've done all I can. I encourage you to have a doctor look at it."

"We'll see how it is tomorrow. I'll have Gideon take a look at it before he heads out. If he falls over from shock, I might go to the clinic in town. Don't worry. We've got hay to put up at Malachi's place. Gideon won't let it turn gangrenous, as he might have to do more of the farmwork."

"Don't joke about it."

"I'll be fine. Especially since you're fixing my shirt."

Gail secured the oversize bandages over the wound as best she could. "Do you have another one to wear in the meantime?"

"Ah, there should be one in my dresser." Samuel stood up from where he'd been perched on the edge of the tub. Overwhelmed by his immediate closeness in the small space, Gail shuffled a step back and stumbled over the toilet behind her. Samuel reached out a hand and grasped her upper arm, catching her before she fell.

"I'll get it." Gail slipped out of his grip toward the door and hastened through it into the living area. Lily skipped over to join her as she crossed the room to hesitate in front of two open doors, one opening into a bedroom, the other leading up some stairs. Glancing back toward the bathroom, Gail saw Samuel at the door. Aware of her dilemma, he nodded her toward the open bedroom door. Entering, she found another spartan room, with only a double bed covered in an old quilt, and a dresser.

She took a moment to marvel at the workmanship of the dresser. If this was something Samuel had made, he had indeed not defaulted to horse-trading because he'd flunked out of furniture-making. It was simple, yet beautiful. As Lily investigated the room, Gail made a guess and pulled a middle drawer open.

Samuel was right. He was getting low on shirts. Gail's fingertips itched at the thought of having the right to make shirts for him. Shaking the sensation, she reached in, pulled out the top one and nudged the drawer shut. With a quick self-conscious stride, she crossed the bedroom and living area, stumbling at the sight of Samuel, his blond head bent as he listened to a chattering Lily, who'd preceded her from the room.

Gail handed him the shirt, then said, "Time to go, Lily-bug." Needing something to do with her hands, she lifted her daughter onto her hip. With the familiar feelings the big, open house evoked and the different ones the man who'd saved her daughter prompted, Gail was glad for the weight and barrier of the little girl.

Unfortunately for Gail's peace of mind, Lily wasn't finished with her conversation. "Do you get to have toys, since you don't have a TV?"

Samuel's lips twitched. "Yes, we have toys. But they're Amish toys and might be a little different than you're used to."

Starting to turn away, Gail paused when

Lily reached out her hands to bracket Samuel's lean cheeks. "I'm going to call you my Amiss man."

Samuel's white teeth were evident in the smile that stretched between her little hands. "I'm honored, Lily."

With a stiff smile, Gail said goodbye and hustled out of the house and across to the truck. Hurriedly, she buckled Lily into her car seat. As she rounded the front of the truck, she waved an arm to a now-shirted Samuel, who'd stepped out of the house. Gail needed to get going. Before she did something foolish, like echoing her daughter's remarks that she'd like to call him her Amish man, too.

Chapter Eight

Gail shielded her eyes with a hand against Friday's late-afternoon sun. The other hand rested on her stomach, pressed against the butterflies that darted there at the sight of a straw-hat-wearing man riding in a cart behind a fast-moving horse. She didn't question that the driver behind the bay was Samuel, not his brother Gideon. She just…knew.

She shouldn't have come. She didn't have any excuse to be here other than the very lame one of returning his shirt. He wasn't expecting her. Yes, she'd made a delivery close by. Somewhat close by. But surely her concern was understandable? The man had gotten hurt protecting her daughter, after all. She'd just wanted to check on how he was doing from his injury earlier this week. Make sure he was healing and taking care of it, which—as her eyes followed his broad back as man and horse started a wide turn—he obviously wasn't.

She could've called. Samuel carried a phone and Gail had his number, but years of culture that prohibited phone use kept her from using the device for extraneous things. Like calling a man you were interested in, just to hear his voice.

Obviously serious about this horse-breaking business, he'd created a makeshift track around a hayfield. When the pair came out of the back turn, Samuel must've seen her, as he swung the horse toward where she stood at the wooden gate.

"Should you be doing this?" She'd waited until he was near enough to hear without shouting.

"I should if I want to know more about a horse that I plan to sell to my neighbors."

"No, I mean, should you be driving with your injured shoulder?"

"Not to be *hochmut*, I am a *gut* driver, but I haven't yet learned to drive with my feet so I have to use my hands and shoulders."

Gail rolled her eyes at the old joke, her nervousness evaporating with his teasing. "You know what I mean."

He secured the reins. Although it was difficult to leave the sight of Samuel's handsome, broad-shouldered figure, when the bay flicked its tail, she darted a glance at it. With relief, she saw that it was the gelding he'd bought that day, not the filly.

Samuel noticed the object of her attention. "Already worked with the filly. Figured I'd rather try her when I was fresher."

"You going to be able to sell her?"

"Without a doubt. She's what I expected. Not as fast as my Belle, but she's fast enough that some might buy her because they'd think so."

"You're not going to race them, are you?" When did she start acting like a mother to more than a three-year-old? Gail shifted uneasily at the possibility that it began when she'd started to care for a certain someone.

"Not where anyone can see." Samuel grinned at her, his blue eyes twinkling.

Gail inhaled deeply, both to forestall her frustration at his recklessness and to settle the bounding butterflies that'd taken flight again at being the recipient of his dazzling attention.

He glanced at the truck parked in the barnyard. "You done for the day?"

My wits are if I can't do anything but bubble and fizz when you look at me like that. "Um, yeah. On my way home."

"Would you like to take a turn with us around the track? It'd give him a feel of different weight in the cart before I try him with the buggy."

Gail's heart rate immediately accelerated as she glanced at the jog cart Samuel sat on. Used for training, it was bigger and bulkier than a racing bike used at the track. Also unlike the racing bike, it had a seat big enough for two. If the two were sitting very close together. Probably not a good idea as the man already made her nervous and was firmly rooted in the Amish world while she and Lily would have to go wherever they could survive together. She pushed back the surge of longing to ride behind a strong trotter in the open air, the ground skimming by beside her and the breeze teasing her face.

Glancing back to his distracting face, Gail opened her mouth to say no, and blinked when a breathless yes came out instead.

Samuel nodded in apparent satisfaction and scooted over the few inches the seat allowed. "You have a stop in the area?"

Gail considered the miles she'd driven out of her way as she stepped forward. "Reasonably close. I brought your shirt back. I'm surprised to see you out working today."

"Why? You're working. Sundays are days

of rest. The rest of the week, there is always much to be done."

For a moment memories of Sundays growing up washed through Gail. Visiting Sundays, spent seeing friends. Church Sundays, where many voices lifted up the songs of the *Ausbund*, before long sermons followed by community dinners and singings in the evening for the *youngies*.

Don't forget the singings where another charming blond man shanghaied your life.

Leave those memories in the past but don't forget their lessons to protect your future. You have enough challenges managing the present. You don't need to add him to them.

"But your back is injured." Standing beside the cart, she again dubiously eyed the narrow seat. Up close, it seemed even smaller.

"Doesn't stop the need for work." Samuel stretched his torso and shifted his shoulders, grimacing fleetingly as he did so. Gail dropped her eyes to the reins in his work-calloused hands. It was safer than his distractingly broad shoulders.

"But now that you mention it, it feels like I've been kicked by a horse."

"How does it look?"

Samuel grunted. "According to Gideon, it looks like a spring sky before a tornado touches down. With blacks, purples and some greenish yellow thrown in."

Gail winced in sympathy, biting her tongue against the offer to check it herself, just to make sure he was okay. Obviously he was, as he reached out a hand to help her into the cart.

Hesitantly, she placed hers in its warm grasp.

"Put your foot there, and there." He guided her into the simple cart. Years ago she'd climbed into many buggies in a dress. It was much easier maneuvering into this one in jeans. An instant later Gail was seated beside him, her hip brushing his. Slowly opening her fingers, she reluctantly released his clasp. She felt him take a breath beside her. "Okay, rest your feet on the bar."

The gelding shifted, taking a step forward. Gail swayed on the seat, shooting out a hand for balance. With no back or sides on the cart, there was nothing to hold on to except…him. She brought her hands to her lap and clenched them, trying to contain her irrational excitement at being in any kind of buggy again.

"Ready?" At her nod, Samuel lifted the reins and urged the gelding forward. The horse took a step and stopped, questioning the unaccustomed load. Samuel gently urged him forward again. The bay's ears twitched and he took another step, gaining confidence as they headed toward the first turn at the end of the field.

"Ready for road gear?" Samuel tossed her a wide smile.

"Do I have a choice?" Gail couldn't help grinning herself.

"Nee!" He signaled to the gelding. They lurched on the seat as the horse sprang into a fast trot. Gail's shoulder bumped Samuel's arm. One hand remaining in her lap, she curled the fingers of the other under the wooden seat to keep steady on her precarious perch.

The gelding might no longer make the time trials, but he was fast. The muffled thud of hooves on the packed dirt of the homemade track was a metronome matching her heart rate. Their speed created a breeze that swept over them, lifting the bay's black tail to stream behind him and causing Gail's ponytail to flutter about the back of her neck. Oh, how she'd missed this! Her smile was probably as wide as the grille on her Dodge.

The ground whizzed by under their feet. Automatically, they both leaned into the curve as the bay swept around it. As they cornered, even bracing her arm, Gail slid toward the outside. Hissing in a breath, she tangled the fingers of her free hand into the rolled-up sleeve of Samuel's shirt to keep herself from slipping off the seat. Once they entered the straight length of the field, she dropped her hand again and edged away a fraction of an inch. She was ready for the second turn.

Samuel eased the gelding into a slower trot as they completed the final turn, approaching the gate where he'd picked her up. "He'll do. He'll do pretty well, in fact. Do you want to drive?" Samuel lifted the reins in her direction.

Gail's fingers itched for the feel of the supple leather. Relinquishing her grip of the seat at the slower pace, she clenched her hands in her lap to keep from reaching for the reins.

"He's got a soft mouth and is well behaved. I'll look for more horses from this trainer." He nodded at the reins in his hand. "Go ahead. See what it feels like to drive a horse instead of your truck. You'll be all right with him, and I'm right here to help you."

Gail glanced over to meet his eyes. Her heart beat heavily. Not because she was afraid. But because she wanted it too much. Uncurling her fists, she reached for the reins.

"Hold them like this."

He cupped her hands in his, guiding the brown leather through her fingers. Gail regretted the loss of the breeze, as she suddenly felt hot all over.

"Okay. Got it?" When he let go, the gelding bobbed its head as if to ask what the holdup was. The reins slid through her hands. Automatically, Gail worked her fingers to gather them up again.

When she glanced at Samuel, he was watching her speculatively. "Ready to go?"

Using her voice and hands, Gail urged the bay ahead, bracing herself for when he surged forward into a fast walk. As they headed into the first turn, Gail clicked the gelding into a faster gait. The gelding drove like a dream, much better than the stubborn Standardbred she'd driven before she left home. She tried to come up with a word to describe her elation as they flew along. The one that came to mind was one she couldn't say. *Wunderbar!*

She asked more speed of him as they raced the quarter-mile length to the back turn of the hayfield. Just as they approached it, a brown figure scurried across the homemade track from the recently cut hay in the center of the field. Gail absently recognized the large marmot as a groundhog. The gelding saw it as a threat. Shying heavily, he jerked Gail halfway off the seat and sent the cart swaying on the uneven ground as he swerved.

Even as Gail instantly and unconsciously regathered control of the horse, she could see

Samuel reach a hand toward the reins to assist her. Before he could do so, Gail regained her seat and smoothly returned the gelding to the track while the marmot hurried across to the tall grass of the fencerow.

When she felt through the leathers that the bay had settled down from his surprise, she gave him a little more rein as they came out of the turn. Samuel had pulled back his hand, but she could feel his attention on her. As they approached the gate, she eased the horse into a slow jog before turning him and walking him back to where she'd gotten into the cart.

Swiveling in the seat toward Samuel, Gail returned the reins to him. "Obviously, he doesn't see many groundhogs on the track, but if I was buying a horse, I'd buy him. That was…" She sucked in a deep breath and blew it out in a long stream. "Thank you."

While his mouth smiled, to her surprise, his eyes did not. "You're a natural. Where'd you learn to drive?"

Gail jerked her hands back into her lap, twisting them into a knot. "Uh, um, when I first worked for George, he let me do a little driving to and from the track."

Samuel nodded. "He taught you well."

"Yeah, I guess." With a weak smile, Gail scrambled from the cart. As Samuel drove the gelding through the gate and to the barn, she walked beside them. He drew the gelding to a halt in front of the big double doors, secured the reins and sprang agilely from the cart.

Facing him, Gail started backing toward her truck. "Thanks again for the ride. I'll… I'll remember it for a long time. And I'm so glad you're feeling better." At his ironic expression, she amended, "Well, maybe not feeling better, but functional at least." Bumping into the rear quarter panel of the Dodge, Gail pivoted and headed for the cab door. By the time she was in and buckled, he was at the driver's window. With reluctant eagerness, Gail rolled it down.

Samuel put his hands on the door when the glass disappeared into it. "I won't be able to get to the track for a bit. There's haying to be done at Malachi's farm." He nodded toward the barn. "And as my operation's still pretty slim, although I enjoy looking, before I buy any more, I need to sell these two. Besides, I have a mare that should be foaling any day now. I need to be here when it arrives in case she has any issues."

A pang shot through Gail at the thought of not seeing him for a while. She cleared her throat. "Take care of your shoulder."

"*Ach, ja.* I'll get it healed in time for the

next kick." Their eyes held a moment before he glanced toward the barn again. "Would you like to know when the mare has her foal? Maybe bring Lily out to see the little fellow?"

"She'd love that." *I would, too. Stop it! He's a distraction, that's all. A mirage that reminds you of what once was and what you thought would be.* Gail turned the ignition. Samuel stepped back when the truck roared to life.

"I'll let you know, then."

"That'd be great. Thanks. Good luck on selling those two." Gail rolled up the window, sealing him out. She wished she could seal him out of her thoughts as easily. Driving down the lane, she adjusted her rearview mirror in order to keep him in view. He hadn't moved from when he'd stepped away from the window. She couldn't see his eyes under his flat-brimmed straw hat, but he seemed to be watching her, as well. Only when she was on the road did she notice something on the seat beside her and realized she still had his shirt. Reaching out a hand, she curled her fingers into the soft fabric.

The truck and trailer pulled out of the lane and accelerated down the road. Samuel turned toward the bay that waited, slouch-hipped, by the barn. Reaching the cart, he bent to un-hitch it and flinched. His back, which the filly had done a good job of irritating when he was driving her today, had been throbbing steadily by the time he worked with the gelding. Up to the time he'd rounded the corner and un-expectedly saw Gail by the gate. At that mo-ment his heart started beating faster than the gelding's quick gait. If he'd been on foot and it'd been a side-by-side competition against the retired track horse, Samuel figured he'd have reached the slender brunette first.

His offer for the drive had generated from his desire to keep her from leaving. And to have her close beside him. He'd been dis-tracted with those sensations. Until she'd handled the Standardbred unerringly and her signature from earlier in the week flashed into his mind.

Abigail Lapp.

With the injury and the inability of getting anything else in his brain other than the feel of her gentle fingers on him since she patched him up in the bathroom, he'd forgotten that feminine scrawl. The offer to drive had acci-dentally become a test. One she'd overwhelm-ingly passed.

Abigail Lapp drove better than some Amish men he knew.

It could be, as she'd said, that she'd learned while working for George at the track. But she was Amish, or had been. He'd eat his straw hat and his winter felt one, too, if she wasn't. From the absolute exuberance on her face during the ride, more joy than he'd seen there since he'd met her, for whatever reason she'd left, she wanted to return now.

Upon leading the unhitched horse into the dim light of the barn, Samuel began removing the harness. For reasons that he wasn't going to examine, it was important to him as well that she return. Slipping the collar from the bay, he remembered Gail's odd response when they'd met Ruth and Hannah Lapp coming down the lane. As he had Gail's face memorized, it wasn't difficult to imagine her bouncy ponytail as blond instead of brunette. The resulting image looked a lot like his sister-in-law's best friend. Although he hadn't paid much mind at church, as they were younger than him, Samuel knew Hannah had a number of brothers. It would be interesting to discover if any of them had dark hair.

Grabbing a brush from its shelf on the wall, he ran it over the gelding. Maybe he'd pay the Lapps a visit. Perhaps they were interested in buying a horse.

Chapter Nine

Another song was started. Voices joined in.
Mainly female voices, as was the norm. Taking a sip from the glass of water in front of
him, Samuel glanced around the room. Other
young men in the room were using the same
excuse to not be singing. Some were talking
quietly with their neighbors, but their attention was on other occupants present. Female
occupants. Behind the glass, Samuel's lips
curved in a slight smile. The young men
didn't come for the singing. They came because the girls were here. The Sunday night
singings were a primary form of accepted
socializing in their community for those in
their *rumspringa*. And the primary purpose
of the *rumspringa* was to find a mate.

His gaze settled on a couple at the end of
the long table. Even though Amish court-

ships were usually kept quiet, all the *youngies* knew that Aaron Raber was walking out with Rachel Mast. Were it not for the fact that Rachel's *daed* was ill and she was needed at home to help on the family farm, theirs would be the first engagement announced come fall. Samuel's attention drifted to a couple of young men standing behind those sitting in chairs at the table. Acknowledging Benjamin, his coworker at the furniture shop, he nodded. When his friend didn't acknowledge him, Samuel looked to see what held the young man's intent interest. Benjamin was staring at his older brother and Rachel. Ach, *looking at a particular woman who's not looking back at you, you're heading for nothing but heartache.*

Samuel's smile twisted before dropping completely. Wasn't he doing the same thing? Setting the glass down, he scrutinized the room again. There were plenty of female smiles aimed at him. Usually the sight and knowledge of the attention encouraged him. Flattered him, in fact, even though he knew it was wrong to be *hochmut*. Maybe that was part of the problem. He'd grown too proud and *Gott* was punishing him for it. Because even though most of the female eyes in the room were focused on him and would love to engage in the verbal dance of arranging to have a ride home, for the first time since he could remember, Samuel couldn't generate any interest in asking.

He lowered his lashes, not wanting to make any eye contact and thereby create any expectations. They almost popped open again at the image that immediately entered his head. A ponytailed dark brunette frowning at him. Gail. His lips curved again. She always started out frowning. Samuel took it as a personal challenge to tease a smile out of her. Most of the time, he succeeded. He got more enjoyment out of a few moments of her snipping at him than he did in an hour of other women concertedly flirting.

His smile faded. He wished he was with her now.

"Something wrong with your drink? Can I get you another?"

Samuel looked up to see a red-haired young woman at his elbow. The singing had stopped and the *youngies* were milling around. There were a few other women behind her, anxiously yet covertly watching, but of course Lydia Troyer was in the lead. He had to admire her tenacity. She'd made a play for Malachi first. Since that'd failed, he was apparently next choice on the menu. Well, this was a time when he'd intentionally follow in his brother's wake.

"*Nee*, the drink is fine."

"The singing isn't to your liking?" The girl was persistent, to say the least.

"*Nee*, just thinking of something else." *Someone* else.

"Something that troubles you, then?" Lydia was acting like she was going to sit down beside him.

"*Ach, ja*, it troubles me." Everywhere he went on the farm and in the house, he thought of Gail, saw her there. In the field, in the house, in his bedroom. Except for the barn; she hadn't been in there yet. But he couldn't spend all his time in the barn trying to find peace from unfamiliar longings for one particular woman.

Samuel pushed up from the table, careful not to bump into the group of girls behind him, all adorned in solid-colored dresses under aprons. "*Ja*. In fact, it requires some heavy thinking." He smiled apologetically to the array of upturned faces under matching *kapps*. "I'm afraid I'm not fit company for anyone tonight." Through the chorus of murmured denials, Samuel made his way to the door. He tried to catch Gideon's eye on the way out, but his brother was too absorbed in his conversation with a young woman. Only seeing the back of her *kapp*, Samuel couldn't identify who she was to tease his *bruder* about later. To his surprise, teasing wasn't the thought that chased through his mind.

Was Gideon serious about a girl? Samuel's brow furrowed at the possibility that his younger *bruder* might get married and settled down before he did. Earlier, he would've laughed and needled him about the situation, while content to divide his own attentions among several girls. But now the possibility made him feel…envious?

Stepping out onto the porch, Samuel closed the door behind him, muting the chattering voices. Striding across the wooden boards, he descended the steps to the sidewalk, his chest rising with a deep inhalation of the night air. He should've thanked his hosts for their hospitality. He'd always made sure to do so before, slipping away briefly from the girl he was driving home that evening. But tonight he didn't pause as he headed where he could see Belle, standing with a cocked hip in the diminishing light.

He was going home from a singing while it was still light outside. Probably the only single male in the community to do so. Certainly the only time he'd done it. What was

the matter with him that he was more interested in a solitary buggy ride home than in
staying to flirt with a bevy of willing young
women?

Gail. It was bad enough that she filled his
senses when he was with her. Even worse that
she filled his mind when he wasn't.

Belle hung her head over the rail from
where she was secured to a post. Samuel
scratched her behind the ear. When he went
to untie her, she reached around to nip at him,
something she hadn't done in months. Distracted, Samuel winced at the pinch on his
biceps before he could jerk away. Fortunately
for him, she hadn't been serious about the
bite.

He rubbed at the wet spot on his sleeve.
"What is it with the females in my life being
so bothersome tonight?" he murmured.

Belle's ears alerted him to the presence behind them. Samuel turned to see that Lydia
had followed him out of the house. Of course.
He usually didn't bother regretting things in
his life, but at the moment, he really regretted that he'd driven Lydia home after a singing one night some weeks back.

"I figured maybe I could distract you from
your troubling thoughts if you gave me a ride

home." The smile on her face indicated she'd had a little practice in being distracting.

Samuel stepped back, closer to the fence and within reach of Belle's teeth. He figured the mare was a safer alternative. Another past action to regret—that he'd kissed the red-headed girl. Although in fairness to him, it hadn't been his idea. He'd just accepted the very obvious invitation to do so.

"That's kind of you to offer, Lydia, but I couldn't ask you to do that." And wouldn't, either. Short of climbing into his buggy—by the look in her eye, he wouldn't put it past her—there wasn't much the girl could do.

Or so he'd thought. When she moved closer, he wasn't so sure.

"It's all right. Maybe you could distract me, too." Reaching out, her hand curled around his biceps.

Samuel shot a glance at the house behind her, the glow from the gaslights inside visible through the windows. Fortunately, the windows didn't contain a silhouette of anyone looking out on what could appear to be an embracing couple.

"*Ach*, you are a distracting woman, Lydia. But my mind is somewhere else and I can't give you the attention you deserve. I don't want to keep some other fortunate fellow from giving you a ride home tonight." Were these his words coming out of his mouth? Samuel almost turned around to see if someone was speaking behind him. Was he really turning down an obvious opportunity to do some kissing?

Shuffling back a foot, he winced when the top board of the fence pressed into his sore shoulder blade. Still, he preferred that over being pressed against the tenacious young woman before him.

Lydia eased in, trapping him against the fence. Her hand slid to his shoulder.

Samuel inhaled. The woman was taking the running-around definition of the *rumspringa* years literally. Just off his ear, Belle snorted. The mare's head was up, white rings showing around her eyes. Samuel figured his eyes were showing a lot of white, as well. It gave him an idea. *Sorry, girl.* Slipping a hand toward the post, he gripped the coarse weave of the rope tethered there and gave it a subtle tug. Belle jerked her head, laid back her ears and bared her teeth. A short foot away, Lydia paused, glancing apprehensively at the mare.

"Careful. She bites."

The warning could apply to both females. When Lydia jumped back, Samuel took the opportunity to deftly hop over the board fence. Shouldering Belle aside, he began untying the bay. It seemed safer to have some type of barrier between him and the redhead. He looked up from his work to see Lydia, now a yard from the fence, eyeing him and the mare doubtfully. Freeing the rope, Samuel patted Belle's sleek neck as they crossed to the gate of the pasture. For the rescue, she'd get an extra measure of oats when they got home. Once through the gate, he gave an intentionally casual wave in Lydia's direction as he headed for the shadowed row of buggies. After a moment of hesitation, the redhead turned toward the house. Two steps in, her pace accelerated.

Samuel heard the closing of the door in the quiet night as he maneuvered Belle between the shafts. Even now, the girl was probably angling for a different ride home. She made him feel old. Only the knowledge that whomever the girl Gideon had been speaking to was he seemed intent about kept Samuel from using the excuse of thanking the evening's host as an opportunity to warn his younger *bruder* about Lydia. Might say a word to Benjamin, though. He didn't want to see a friend tied to the girl for life. Men could sometimes be fools for flirty eyes and smiling lips.

Securing a trace to the shaft, he paused, visualizing eyes, more wary than flirty, meeting his. *Ach*, men could sometimes be fools for those, as well. At least he was.

Was he a fool? He shouldn't even be thinking of her in that way. Gail was living in the *Englisch* world, while he didn't plan on leaving the Plain community. He had to tread carefully. He needed her freight service for his business. He was barely making a profit as it was. Although Malachi was a decent boss, Samuel didn't want to have to go hat in hand back to work for him.

As for his disturbing *Englisch* driver, he'd taken a close look at the Lapp family during church and over the noon meal today. He'd made a point to visit with Zebulun— who was brown haired, as were some of his sons. Automatically finishing his task, Samuel absently leaned against Belle. The Lapps all had blue eyes, similar to a pair that continually haunted him.

Although tempted to do so, Samuel hadn't pried or gossiped about their family history. He didn't need to. He was certain they had a daughter named Gail who'd left the Amish community for some reason, probably because she'd been unmarried and with child. She'd managed to live in the *Englisch* world for years. She might never want to return.

And he shouldn't try to convince her. But *ach*, the prospect was appealing. Would it be wrong? She seemed lonely for family and needed help with Lily. Besides *Gott*, there was nothing more important than family for the Amish.

Belle stomped a foot and shifted away from him.

"Easy there," he soothed as he gathered the reins and took them back to the buggy. Climbing in, he acknowledged he needed to take his own advice. He needed to take it easy. Not push her. Let Gail choose what she wanted in life. But his agile mind started thinking about how he could solve her problems and help his, as well.

Adjusting the leathers in his hands, Samuel lifted the brake, slightly disturbed at how much he wanted Gail to decide that what she wanted included him.

Gail pulled into the lane, her attention on Lily's chatter behind her. Her daughter was thrilled at the prospect of seeing a baby horse. Samuel had called to advise that a foal had been born on Monday. It was hard to tell who was more excited: Lily to see the foal, or Gail to see the foal's owner. But whereas Lily could express her enthusiasm, Gail wouldn't

have done so even if she could've. She tried
to suppress her own eagerness.

Focused on the barn, she didn't notice the
Amish buggy and bay tethered by the house
until she'd parked the truck and Lily was already fumbling with her seat belt. Upon seeing the rig, Gail's hands automatically went
to the ignition to start the truck again and
escape. Fingers squeezing the key, she hesitated, sick at heart of the constant fear and her
propensity to run. She'd been fearful and running for four years. Running from her family
and community because of fear and shame.
Barely outrunning destitution. Falling behind
in bills. Being swallowed up by loneliness. *I
used to be brave. I used to be cheerful. What
happened to that Gail?* Still, she began to
twist the key head. It could be anyone in the
Amish community, but she couldn't take the
risk.

Too late. Through the windshield, Gail saw
Samuel coming out of the barn, followed by
two women wearing *kapps* and dresses covered by aprons. Gail froze at the sight of the
smiling blonde walking beside the shorter
red-haired woman.

"Come on, Mommy! Let's go see!" Lily
had wiggled out of her seat and was tugging
at the door handle.

Gail reached a hand between the seats and rested it on her daughter's back. Panting, it took her a moment before she could speak. "Just a minute, sweetie. Um, let Mommy come around and get you, okay?" The numb fingers of her left hand curled around the front door handle. Samuel must've seen her face, because, before she gave the handle a tug that would change her life, she saw his charming smile fade and a look of concern drop over his handsome features. One tinged with anticipation. And guilt.

He hadn't planned this, had he? How could he have known? How could he have done such a thing? Cold sweat beaded down Gail's back as her stomach twisted at the thought of being betrayed again by a handsome Amish man.

"Let's get out, Mommy!" Lily tugged at the door handle again. A muffled click heralded her success in getting it open. Before Gail could stop her, Lily scrambled down from the truck and ran around to the front of it.

It took three tries before Gail could get her door open. She hung on to it for support when she climbed out. Lily, impatient with her mother's delay, ran to her, grabbed Gail's hand and pulled her forward.

Obviously, the blonde woman wasn't party to any preplanned arrangement. Stumbling to a halt, her rounded blue eyes never left Gail's face. Her lips parted as her jaw sagged. For a moment she uttered no sound. Then joy broke over her lovely features like she'd just been given her heart's desire and she surged forward, voicing the name Gail never figured she'd be called again.

"Abigail?"

Chapter Ten

Gail remained planted in front of the truck as surely as if she'd taken root there. When she didn't move or speak, the wonder on Hannah's face faded to be replaced with uncertainty. Her sister slowed before stopping a few yards away.

"We were so worried about you. Why didn't you write? Any kind of message. Just to know that you were alive and well would've meant so much." Hannah's words were barely above a whisper.

Gail's lips trembled. "I couldn't," she finally got out. "It would've been too hard."

"You know I would've helped you any way I could've."

"I know." Gail rolled her lips inward and bit them. The hurt on her sister's face devastated her. "I... I just had to make a clean break. If

I'd written to you, I…" She sniffed sharply. "I couldn't have done it. I would've had to come back. But I couldn't, because of…" Her eyes dropped to her daughter, who stood uncharacteristically silent beside her.

Hannah's eyes dropped to Lily, as well. "Is this…?" Her hands came up to steeple against her mouth.

Gail nodded. Gently grasping Lily's shoulders, she shifted the little girl to stand before her. "This is my daughter, Lily. Lily, I'd like you to meet…" Her voice drifted off. How did she explain to Lily that she had an aunt, her mommy's sister who'd never been mentioned? And where could it go from there? Gail still couldn't come back to the community. Not with the risk of losing Lily. Clearing her throat, she continued, "Lily, this is Hannah, a good friend of Mommy's from when she was a little girl." Gail's nose prickled against unshed tears. She was being so unfair. Hannah had certainly been that, but she was also so much more.

Hannah flinched at the deception as her eyes lifted to meet Gail's. Drawing a deep breath, she knelt to Lily's level and did what Hannah always did best. Gracefully composing herself, she made the others around her comfortable. "Hello, Lily. How are you? Your *mamm* is right. I knew her before you were born. I'm so glad to meet you because—" although Hannah smiled brightly, she paused on a little hiccup of air "—I've always wondered about you."

Gail relaxed her fingers from their stiff grip on Lily's shoulders as the girl stepped forward. "How did you know my mommy?"

"We grew up together." Hannah glanced again to Gail and smiled more naturally. "She was my best friend."

"Really?" Lily stepped closer. "My best friend is Miss Patty."

Gail crossed her arms over her chest at the stab that shot through her at her daughter's admission that her best friend was the fifty-something woman who watched her during the day. Lily didn't have any playmates her own age. No siblings. Didn't attend any community frolics where kids ran and interacted with those their age. What a lonely life for a child. Her daughter should have more friends.

"Miss Patty must be very wonderful to have a good friend like you."

"She is. We bake and color and go to the store and watch TV." Lily now stood a foot away from Hannah, who lifted her arms like she wanted to embrace the child, before carefully returning them to her lap.

"I like to bake, as well."

"What's on your head?"

Hannah reached up to the pleated organdy that covered her hair. "This? It's called a *kapp*. I wear it when I pray, and since I am to pray without ceasing, I always have it on."

"I have a purple hat. Would you like to wear it for a while?"

Hannah smiled, a sweet expression that enhanced her gentle beauty. "That's very generous of you to offer, but I've grown used to this one and while I might struggle to put your purple one on, I'm sure it's a perfect fit for you."

Lily giggled. "Samuel put it on and he looked funny."

"My dignity is under attack here." Samuel stepped forward from where he and the red-haired woman Gail recognized as Ruth Fisher had stopped outside the barn's open double doors. His watchful gaze shifted between Gail and Hannah before he spoke to Lily. "Hey, Lily, would you like to see the foal?"

"Yes!" Lily skipped over to him and, without hesitation, reached for his hand. They disappeared into the shadows of the barn, Ruth Fisher, now Schrock, turning to join them. Gail had felt the woman's eyes on them, as well. No doubt the intention of the two adults entering the barn was to give her and Hannah some time alone.

Glancing at her sister, she found Hannah watching her, a slight, compassionate smile on her lips, but a wary look in her blue eyes.

Gail didn't know what to do with her hands. First tightening them across her chest, she then dropped them to her sides before crossing them over her chest again. She felt like she was flying apart at the bombardment of emotions. She wanted to run to her sister, shouting with joy at seeing her again. Giggle together as they used to do as young girls. Cry with happiness at meeting someone from her family once again. Cry with fear at the repercussions this meeting might bring. Four years of facing life alone left her braced in front of the truck, rubbing her hands along her upper arms.

And Hannah, sweet Hannah, seemed to understand her dilemma. She rose to her feet. "You are looking well."

"Thanks. You, too," Gail replied stiffly.

They stared at each other a moment before Hannah nodded to Gail's jeans. "Are they as comfortable as everyone says?"

For the first time since she'd seen the buggy in the yard, Gail had the urge to smile. "Hotter in the summertime than a dress, but easier to get around in for some things."

"I always envied our *brieder* for their ability to wear pants when we did chores in the wintertime. I wonder if they envied me for being able to wear dresses in the heat of the summer."

Now Gail's numb lips did stretch into a smile. "I doubt it. They were probably thinking instead about escaping to the pond to go swimming." Her smile ebbed and she drew a ragged breath. "How are they? How are *Mamm* and *Daed*?"

"All well. Our *brieder* have grown so much you'd hardly recognize them. Jonah is a few years into his *rumspringa*, with Josiah just about to start. *Mamm* and *Daed*—" Hannah paused and sighed. "They miss you. I missed you. I know why you didn't say goodbye. But it hurt them."

"I couldn't. If I had, I wouldn't have had the strength to go."

"I know." Hannah looked toward the barn before returning her eyes to Gail. "She's *wunderbar*. *Mamm* would be so thrilled to have a *kinskind*."

Gail nodded as her face crumbled. "I'm so sorry," she sobbed.

In two strides, they were in each other's

arms, both laughing and crying simultaneously. Gail almost wept anew at the feel of being the center of someone's embrace. Of being supported instead of always being the support. She hadn't allowed herself to cry like this since years before when she was in Hannah's arms, sobbing after she'd heard Atlee and Louisa's betrothal announced at church and knowing that left her with child and alone. When Gail's ragged breathing steadied, she held her sister a moment more before grasping Hannah's forearms and stepping back.

"I've knocked your *kapp* awry. I've never seen you out without it being pinned perfectly."

"It's probably knocked askew because all the prayers I've prayed while wearing it have been answered. Well, most of them anyway."

Releasing Hannah's arms, Gail slid the back of her hand under her nose. Hannah linked her elbow with Gail's and led her into the shade at the side of the barn. "Our faces look about the same as the day you left. I watched you until I couldn't see you anymore. From what I'd heard in the community, no one saw you leave Miller's Creek. What happened?"

"I was so afraid that someone I knew

would see me walking down the road. But after about a mile, a passing *Englisch* woman, fortunately not a neighbor, stopped. I told her some tale of going to visit my cousins in Indiana. She took me to the bus stop. From there, I got on a bus to Milwaukee."

"Why not Madison?"

"Too close. I knew Madison would be too tempting to come home and relatively easy to get a ride from there when things got hard." Gail paused a moment, remembering how hard things had gotten. Even being very careful, she'd quickly burned through her meager savings from part-time jobs working at a vegetable stand and waitressing at the Dew Drop restaurant. She blinked away the memory. That was in the past. If they didn't lose the truck and trailer, she and Lily would survive. Somehow.

"Anyway, being farther away was better. You said no one saw me leave?"

Hannah shook her head, but her smile faded.

"But things were said, weren't they?"

Hannah leaned back against the weathered white paint of the barn. "It's amazing how much talking about someone gets done when we all know gossiping is a sin."

Gail folded her arms across her chest and

waited. It was what she'd expected, after all. She widened her eyes against tears that threatened over what her parents must have gone through after her abrupt and secretive departure. A bitter taste of remorse filled her mouth.

"*Ja*, there was talk. It hurt *Mamm* and *Daed*, but not as much as it hurt them having you gone. I hope that you'll see them and let them know you're all right?" Apparently interpreting Gail's set face, Hannah sighed softly. "I don't know what was going on with Ruby Weaver, but she wasn't very kind."

Gail snorted, remembering some of the things the bishop's wife had said to her. "That's her nature."

"I think hurt people hurt people."

Gail's lips twisted. The woman must be very pained indeed. A bit of it, she could understand. A large family was considered a great blessing to the Amish. Ruby Weaver only had one living son. Still, Gail recalled past situations in the community where questionable rules had been enforced that punished some while benefiting others. "Are all bishops like this?"

Hannah's brows furrowed before she shook her head. "I don't think so. Our leaders are chosen by lot. Some seem to handle the responsibility better than others. I correspond with someone in another district and she writes very highly of their bishop." Hannah hesitated a moment. "I heard…" Her voice trailed off and she glanced away.

When her *schweschder* didn't continue, Gail dropped her arms and took a step forward. "What? What is it? You're still as readable as a book, Hannah."

Meeting Gail's intent gaze, Hannah began again with obvious reluctance. "Bishop Weaver stopped by the farm shortly after you left. I was in the milk house, but I heard him telling *Daed* that if any gossip was spread about how Atlee might have…*treated* you, he would know where it started and would ensure our family regretted it."

Gail's fingernails cut into her palms as she clenched her fists. It was what she'd feared. "Any threat against her favored son would've come straight from Ruby. *Daed* and *Mamm* would never say anything, but they can't control how the community talks."

Hannah winced. "I keep expecting the Weavers to become more compassionate, but since Atlee died they seem to have only gotten worse."

Gail frowned. "What happened to Atlee and Louisa's *boppeli*? I know there was one, as Louisa was…more evident than I was when I left."

"I think the whole community knew she was with child. Ruby seemed as happy as anytime I've known her. The couple never made their public confessions of sin, but there were subtle signs of an accelerated wedding to accommodate the situation. I would imagine, given a choice, Ruby wouldn't have agreed. But other women of the community would have none of her son being the exception when Ruby had ensured over the years that any other expectant couples' weddings were somewhat slighted.

"As for the *boppeli*…" Hannah shook her head. "I don't know. Shortly after they got married, Louisa was ill and in the hospital. The community held fund-raising frolics to help pay the bills. There was no *boppeli*. And there's been no *boppeli* in the two years she's been married to Atlee's older *bruder*."

Gail sucked in a breath. No other *boppeli* meant Lily was the Weavers' only grandchild. It was worse than she thought.

She tried to distract herself with Hannah's last statement. It was news to Gail that Atlee's widow had married his older brother. She didn't know Jethro Weaver well. Several years older, although unmarried, he hadn't interacted with the *youngies* when she'd been in the community. Already baptized, he'd hung out with the married men. As opposed to his charismatic and outgoing younger *bruder*, Jethro had been quiet and withdrawn.

"You know how it goes. After a while something else comes up for people to talk about." Slanting a teasing smile at Gail, Hannah tipped her head toward the double doors of the barn. "He's created quite a stir in the community, at least for the young women. He and his *brieder*."

Gail's gaze slid to where Samuel and Lily had disappeared a while ago. Her mouth firmed into a thin line. The reasons the women might be interested in the attractive Schrock *brieder* were obvious. But all Gail could think of was that the man had manipulated her via her daughter to come here today. Which made him untrustworthy. Just like the man who'd caused her to leave the community years ago.

"He's little! And fuzzy!" Lily pointed a finger to the spindly-legged foal peeking around her mother's tail at the back of the wooden stall.

"He's a she. A girl, which makes her a filly." Samuel steadied Lily from where she perched on the rail by the manger.

"I'm a girl. Am I a filly?"

"No, that's what a young girl horse is called."

"I'd like to be a horse."

Samuel touched a finger to her nose. "I'm not surprised, but you're *wunderbar* the way you are."

"Does she have a name?"

"Not yet. I've been trying to think of a special one."

"Can I name her? She could be Princess. Or Brownie."

"Those are both good names, but giving a special name takes time." He lifted her from the rail to set her down outside the stall. "You go home and think of some possibilities. We'll discuss them next time I see you."

"Okay," Lily agreed over her shoulder as she scampered over to get acquainted with the orange-and-white barn cat. As the cat was a friendly one, and Lily looked like she'd had some experience as a cat petter, Samuel rested his elbows on the stall's top rail, facing the barn's open double doors. No one was in view outside, but Ruth made her presence known beside him.

His sister-in-law stood with hands on her slender hips, bracketing her apron and the slight bump underneath it. "Now I know why you invited me here at this specific time and urged me to bring Hannah. I thought for a moment that you'd had the good sense to be interested in Hannah. I almost warned her off you, but I knew I didn't have to because Hannah has more sense than to be interested in you." Ruth's green eyes narrowed. "But it's not Hannah you're interested in, is it? It's her sister. Who's now *Englisch*. She didn't know about this little arrangement, did she?"

When Samuel silently shifted his stance in response, Ruth slid her hands off her hips and shook her head. "I don't know what your game plan was, but this might not end up quite the way you expected."

Samuel was thinking the same thing. From the look on Gail's face when she'd spotted Hannah accompanying him from the barn, he'd been surprised a plume of dust hadn't followed the speeding truck down his lane. It was far from the joyous reaction he'd anticipated.

He inhaled sharply as the sunlight through the door silhouetted two figures entering. As they were arm in arm, he took it as a good sign.

Lily noted her mother and, leaving the cat, ran to her. "Mommy! I saw a filly! It's a girl horse. I want to be one, but Samuel says I'm okay as I am."

Gail picked up her daughter and settled

her on her hip. "That you are, sweetheart."
She shot a look at Samuel. It wasn't nearly
as friendly and welcoming. Neither was her
tone of voice as she added, "We both are."

Samuel straightened from his slouch
against the stall. He flinched when Ruth
clapped her hands together a single time before striding over to mother and daughter.

"Lily, I have a girl horse, too. She's older,
so she's called a mare. Her name is Bessie.
She's a grouchy old girl, but would you like
to meet her? And maybe sit in the buggy she
pulls for me?"

Lily scrambled down from her mother's
arms. "Yes. I like horses."

"*Gut.* And we'll take your new friend, Hannah, with us." With an Amish woman on either side of the little girl, they strolled out of
the barn.

Never had Samuel appreciated his sister-in-
law more. He wanted to step closer to Gail,
but her posture warned against it.

"You used my daughter to manipulate us
into coming today. Did I ever give you any
indication that I wanted to have more contact with the Amish community?" Apparently
seeing the answer on his face, she continued,
"I didn't think so."

Samuel drew in a deep breath. "I thought it

would make you happy. I see how much you struggle. I see how hard it is parenting Lily without family and I wanted to help you, because I—because that's what we do in the Amish community."

"How did you know?"

He didn't ask what she meant. "I saw your name the other day and guessed from your reaction the day Ruth and Hannah came down the lane. Also, you're a very *gut* driver for just a few lessons." Samuel tried a teasing smile but scrapped it when he saw how Gail's hands were trembling.

"You should've asked me first."

"I figured Lily needed a family."

Gail went rigid at that. "Lily has me." She shook her head. "You don't understand what you've done."

"I wanted to help."

"You can help by paying attention to what I want for my daughter. When you do the exact opposite, it shows that you feel your opinion is above mine. I have no problem with that when it's in regard to your life, but when it's about mine, it's hurtful and shows a lack of respect for me. And also shows that I can't trust you with things that are important to me."

Gail wrapped her arms around herself, like she was cold in the summer heat of the barn.

"It's probably a good thing, as I was beginning to trust you. Maybe you did me a favor. I needed a reminder not to let a man hurt me again. Or, worse, hurt Lily. This isn't some kind of flirtation, this is our lives. My world turned upside down when I learned I couldn't trust a man I was…" She stopped abruptly before going on hoarsely. "I can't trust you. I should have known better once I saw your handsome face."

Samuel was stung. This was far from the dulcet tones and flirtatious smiles he got when he did something to please a woman. "I was only trying to help."

"I don't need this kind of help." Spinning on her heel, Gail strode for the door.

Dropping his head back to stare at the weathered gray boards of the hayloft above, Samuel inhaled deeply. Why couldn't Gail understand that he'd done it for her? Her and Lily. When he looked toward the door again, she was gone. He kicked at a chunk of straw that'd dropped from a bale, creating a shower of golden stalks. The mare and foal watched him warily from the back of the stall.

Ach. Chagrined at himself, Samuel crooned to the pair until they settled down, forcing himself to do so, as well. *Ja,* he'd done it for Gail, but hadn't he done it for himself, as well? Because for reasons he couldn't explain, he wanted her to return to the Amish community. What if she wouldn't haul horses for him anymore? It was entirely possible. He grimaced. Although it would cut into the slim profits of his growing business, he could find someone else to transport his horses. But could Gail find hauls to replace the revenue she'd lose? He knew she needed the money.

Striding to the wall of the barn, Samuel grabbed the pitchfork that hung there before he marched across the barn to muck out Jeb's and Huck's stalls. If that didn't take the edge off his righteous energy, he'd find another physical task to do. Farming was full of them. Good thing summer evenings were long because it would take a lot of daylight to work off his frustration.

Chapter Eleven

Samuel rubbed at the grime in the leather, his ears tuned in for the sound of a large engine coming down the road. Keeping harnesses in good shape took maintenance. But today the job was more for him to be occupied than for the leather to stay in condition.

He hoped she'd come. He hoped she'd taken the job. If she hadn't…

Thoughts of their conversation in the barn on Thursday afternoon had distracted him for the past few days. Initially hurt and affronted by Gail's reprimand, by Thursday night he'd been honest enough to acknowledge there'd been some truth in what she'd said. It'd been obvious by her reserved behavior that privacy was important to her. If she'd wanted to interact with Hannah, she certainly wouldn't have hidden herself behind sunglasses and a

hat and slunk so far down behind the wheel
that she was barely visible.

He'd been a fool. An arrogant fool to think
he knew better than what Gail obviously
wanted. And it cost him what he was realizing that he wanted.

By Friday morning Samuel was thinking
of ways to apologize to Gail, or at least as-
certain that they could still do business together if nothing else. Calling her would've
been fruitless—it would be too easy for her
to ignore. He knew she lived somewhere reasonably close, but he didn't know where. He
thought about asking Hannah if she knew, but
as he'd already muddied that up, he thought
better of it.

Which was why this morning he'd gone
to an auction. He'd approached Malachi and
Gideon with the need for more draft horses
for their two farms. Jeb and Huck were eager
and hardworking, but the farms were more
than the two Belgians could handle alone. In
fact, it was past time to increase their horsepower, as they'd had to borrow horses already
for some of the work. And if the two geldings
he bought today were on the far reaches of
their community, far enough out that the new
purchases would need to be hauled home,

well, he knew a good buy when he saw it. He was a horse trader, after all.

He'd paid in advance for the transportation, arranging that the auction barn would contact a hauler, specifically Gail, to deliver the animals. Samuel only hoped that she took the job. If she transported the horses, maybe it was a sign she'd forgiven him. Surely Gail still had enough Amish in her to practice the principle of forgiveness? Or maybe she'd take the job because she really needed the money. Hate him she might, but she was a practical woman. Either way, he could see her and apologize.

Samuel jerked his head toward the barn door at the rumble of a motor and the muted rattle of a trailer under a heavy load. Dropping the leather on the counter as he strode out of the tack room toward the barn's double doors, he willed it to be a black pickup coming up the lane, even if its brown-haired driver refused to talk with him.

His shoulders sagged in relief at the sight of the familiar rig pulling into the farmyard. Through the windshield he could see Gail's composed face. It revealed no trace of their emotional conversation. Circling the yard, she backed the rear of the trailer toward the barn doors. Clanks rang through the trailer as his new purchases stomped their bucket-sized feet.

When the trailer stopped, Samuel went to work opening the gate, all senses on alert should Gail come into view. Would she stay in the truck and leave him to unload the Belgians by himself? It was entirely possible.

She didn't.

"I don't suppose Mr. Klopfenstein just happened to have my name and number." When Samuel swung open the gate, Gail stepped inside to untie the first gelding from the trailer's modified setup to handle the oversize passengers.

"It's possible. You worked with Elam and have a growing reputation." Samuel held the gate wide to avoid a repeat of last week. Draft horses were normally gentle, but they were huge. It was difficult for anyone to handle a ton of excited animal and he didn't know the personalities of these geldings.

"Possible, but not probable. Where do you want this big fella?"

"Going to let them settle down outside." When Gail cleared the back of the trailer, Samuel strode over to open a gate along the white fence that lined the pen next to the barn. He'd already moved Jeb and Huck to a lot behind the barn until he had a chance to get everyone acquainted.

While she was leading the first gelding through the gate, he returned to the trailer to get the second. Once they were both inside the pasture, Samuel closed the gate. His charge had his head and tail up, looking around his new home. The gelding was so tall the top of Samuel's hat just barely reached the Belgian's throatlatch, where the horse's head joined its neck. Samuel looked over to see Gail's arm fully extended as she held her horse.

"Go ahead and release him," Samuel directed as he freed his own. The Belgian swung away to trot across the pasture, quickly joined by the other gelding. Drawing in a long breath, Samuel waited while Gail walked toward him. Now that they didn't have four thousand pounds of horseflesh between them, it was time to apologize.

"They're magnificent, aren't they?" Her eyes were on the giant chestnuts trotting along the far fence.

Samuel watched the horses' excited explorations, as well. "I think so."

"You did it again, you know." When he returned his attention to Gail, she was still looking at the Belgians. He couldn't read anything from her expression.

"You manipulated me to do what you wanted."

Samuel closed his eyes and leaned back against the fence as the realization stabbed through him. "*Ach*, you're right. I'm sorry. I wanted to see you and I didn't know if you would want the same. And I thought the money from the haul would help."

"It does. But I'm trying to figure out if the right action for the wrong reason makes the action right or wrong."

Samuel opened his eyes, awaiting his judgment. "Which way are you leaning?"

With a sigh, Gail turned to meet his gaze. "Although you should've figured out that I'd have contacted my family if I'd have wanted to, I didn't tell you that I specifically was trying to avoid them. So I guess I have to give you another chance." Her lips hooked in a self-mocking smile. "Besides, I need your business and your money."

Relaxing more heavily against the fence, Samuel sighed, as well. "I'm glad." He returned her smile. "And likewise, in reverse." Exceedingly relieved that she had a forgiving nature, he studied her face a moment. She seemed calm. Maybe it was safe to ask. "Why?"

She didn't answer for a while. The way

she perused him in return, Samuel knew she was trying to determine if giving him another chance meant trusting him, as well. When she finally did speak, Gail didn't try to prevaricate. "Why didn't I want to see them? Partly because I'm ashamed. I made a mistake. A big one. Partly a bit of fear that they'll resent Lily. What if they won't accept her? She's my daughter. I'll fight like a… Well, Amish might be a nonviolent society, but mamas still will protect their babies." Gail smiled without mirth. "But mostly because I knew it'd be too hard to continue to stay away once I'd contacted them. I feared it'd create the little crack in the dam that eventually brings the whole barrier down."

He furrowed his brow. "If you want to come home, why do you have to stay away in the *Englisch* world?"

"Because if I come back, I might lose Lily."

Samuel abruptly straightened from the fence. "What? Why?"

Gail shook her head as she regarded him. "How many unwed Amish mothers do you see in the community?"

Blinking, Samuel searched his memory for the various community members he'd met or heard about since they'd arrived. The only single mothers he could come up with were widows. He didn't say anything. The Amish were a forgiving society, but there were certain expectations regarding behavior.

"Exactly." Gail read his face. "I think the community would accept them, or some would at least." Gail crossed her arms in front of her. "But probably not in my case." Her eyes were fixed on the geldings. Having explored the perimeters of the pasture, they were settling down to graze. "I don't know why I'm telling you this. Probably because I'm so…tired of not talking with someone. Tired of running away. And you made me face the past."

She glanced at Samuel before returning her attention to the horses. "I was a fool when I began my *rumspringa*. I wanted to find *Gott*'s chosen one for me. But I was too *hochmut* to let Him do the choosing. I never gave Him a chance. I went for the good-looking, sweet-talking fellow who paid attention to me." She slanted Samuel a droll look. He returned it with a wince and a crooked smile as he recognized himself.

"I'd heard things about him that weren't… flattering. But to me, he was. Very much so. He told me everything an awkward girl with a beautiful older sister wanted to hear. I thought that meant he cared for me. He might not have been *Gott*'s, but he was my chosen one. And so I…did things I shouldn't have." Gail looked back at the grazing horses.

"A short while later I discovered I was with child." She shook her head. "I was so excited. I was going to tell Atlee after church that Sunday, figuring it meant we would get married soon. Before I had a chance to, the deacon announced that Atlee was betrothed. To the girl he'd been walking out with before he turned his eye to me." Gail snorted. "I barely made it out of the Zooks' barn before I was ill."

Again, Samuel searched his memory, this time with a twinge of something—surely not jealousy—for an Atlee among the young men he knew in the community. He came up blank. But he'd heard the name. Narrowing his eyes, he tried to recall where and when it'd been mentioned. He inhaled deeply when it came to him. "The bishop's son who fell during a barn-raising?"

Grimacing, Gail nodded. "Yes. I heard about his fall from Elam."

"The bishop's son," Samuel repeated flatly. "Do you know Bishop Weaver and his wife, Ruby?"

"Haven't met his wife. Met the bishop a time or two. He was the one who wouldn't let

Ruth keep her *daed*'s furniture shop, which is what brought us to Miller's Creek. After which, Malachi and Ruth met and ended up getting married. I guess that makes the bishop something of a matchmaker." The last was said tonelessly. Samuel felt like he'd taken a blow to the stomach. It was one thing to know Gail had a daughter. It was another to hear her tell of falling for another man. And how he'd treated her. The bishop's son.

A bishop, by enforcing the *Ordnung*, held considerable influence over a community. Some were fair and rational; some not so much. Bishop Weaver fell more into the latter category. Although Amish chose to live life a certain way to be closer to *Gott*, they were still humans. Humans who sometimes let power and control go to their heads. He was beginning to see Gail's dilemma.

Gail couldn't imagine the stern bishop as a matchmaker. As for the bishop's wife, well, the prospect was impossible. She'd done a lot of thinking in the past few days. Seeing Hannah had made her realize she'd never be whole or happy without some of her family in her life. If she wasn't whole, how could she be the mother that Lily needed? What was she doing to her daughter to narrow her life so? Could she see her family and still avoid the bishop's wife?

"I guess that was the silver lining for me. Not having them as in-laws." A mother-in-law who'd thought of her as the worst sort of jezebel. Gail didn't know what Ruby Weaver had seen or been told of their secret rendezvous, but the thought of how foolish she'd been in her infatuation for the older and charming Atlee made her flush with shame. Her remorse was quickly followed by a flash of anger that Ruby had thought less of Gail's family, even going so far as to threaten them when her son was at least partially at fault.

"So when my…situation was getting too much to hide, I left."

"I understand it would be difficult, but why would you lose Lily if you returned?"

"The Amish society is based on *gelassenheit*. Yielding oneself to a higher authority. The welfare of the community is more important than individual rights and choices." Gail's mouth twisted as Samuel acknowledged what she said with a nod. "I know the bishop and his wife would ensure it deemed necessary in the community for Lily to be raised by a two-parent family instead of a single mother, especially one who's been *Englisch* for some years. And from what I learned from Hannah,

I even know who the family would be. Jethro Weaver and his wife are childless. This way, Ruby could manipulate things so she'd end up with her own grandchild without everyone knowing of Atlee's and my shame." Gail rolled in her lips to keep them from trembling.

"Not your shame." Samuel's words were adamant, and opposite of the compassionate look he gave her.

Now Gail's chin trembled, as well. "I thought he loved me. I was such a weak fool."

"You were young. He shouldn't have done what he did." Reaching out a finger, Samuel tipped up her chin. "You are an incredibly strong woman." When he opened his arms, it was the most natural movement in the world to be gathered into his warmth and strength.

Leaning her head against his chest, Gail relaxed for what felt like the first time in over four years. She didn't know if she fully trusted Samuel, but at the moment, she needed him.

She'd wanted to stay angry with him. But she couldn't. He was right. It'd been too good to see Hannah again.

When today's haul opportunity arose, she'd known it wasn't an accident. That Samuel was behind it. Yes, she'd needed the money, but just as much, she'd wanted to see him again.

"I can understand why she wants a grand-child." Gail spoke into the center of his shirt. She didn't know if he could even hear her. "But I'm not giving up my daughter."

Samuel's arms tightened around her. "She won't get Lily."

Tears prickled at the backs of Gail's eyes at his flat statement. She'd spent years without anyone in her corner. She'd been afraid that if she told Samuel of her history, it would drive him away, but the opposite seemed to be true. The notion gave her courage to bring up something else that'd been troubling her for the past few days.

"Speaking of a *grossmammi*, Hannah thinks I should bring Lily to meet my parents. Or at least come and see them myself. So they know I'm all right."

She felt his chest rise under her cheek as he took a deep breath. "What do *you* want to do?"

Gail closed her eyes and just let herself be held against the steady beat of his heart for a moment. She wanted to do what she'd always wanted to do. Be with her family. But should she? What of the repercussions to her and Lily if she opened that door? Once would not be enough. She took strength again in his supportive statement.

"I want to introduce Lily to my family. But

I'm scared. It's been so long. I didn't tell them I was leaving. It would've been too hard to go, then." Gail leaned back in his arms. His blue eyes, usually so flirtatious, were solemn when they met hers. "What if they don't want to see me?"

"They will." When she nodded hesitantly, mutely, his customary glint returned. "Abigail, huh?"

Gail's lips twitched. "I want you to go with me."

"What?"

"I want you to go with Lily and me when we see my folks. Another person around to dispel the awkwardness in case it doesn't work out."

"I'm not family."

"But you got me into this. So you're going to be there." When Gail stepped back, Samuel loosened his embrace, but didn't fully release her, sliding his hands down her arms to cup her elbows. Gail relished the continued connection.

Samuel's gaze flicked out into the pasture, where he watched the Belgians for a moment before returning to her. She saw his throat work as he swallowed. "All right."

Later, in the truck driving home, Gail knew Samuel could be trusted to be there.

But could she trust the feelings she was beginning to have for him? Could she trust her ability to protect Lily if something went wrong? She was barely keeping a roof over their heads now as it was. But the door to home had been opened and she couldn't resist peeking through it.

Chapter Twelve

Samuel knew he was nervous when Belle stopped fighting him and started flicking her ears back toward him in confusion. Usually the mare was high-strung enough for both of them, but today she was surprisingly calm, or at least confused by the tension that ran down the lines from his hands to her mouth. Samuel didn't know if he wanted Belle to keep up her ground-eating stride and arrive sooner in case Gail needed him the moment she pulled into the Lapp farm, or slow her trot, delaying his arrival until after the emotional gathering. After their conversation the previous day, he was almost as anxious about the reunion as she was.

How would the Lapps take his presence? It wasn't like he and Gail had an understanding that might justify it. Samuel's pulse jumped at the thought. Previously, anytime a girl he was seeing mentioned commitment, or broadcasted that they were together, he went out of his way to ensure they no longer were.

Fingering Belle's reins, he searched for any temptation to flee. And was surprised to find none. More surprised to discover that he was glad to be there for Gail and Lily. To take his cues from Gail. If she needed him to forestall an ugly situation, he was ready to step in. If she needed him to give her an excuse to leave promptly, he'd provide that, as well.

Gail wanted to arrive during milking time. Before she left yesterday, she'd said she felt more comfortable showing up when her family would be distracted by chores, hoping they'd be less likely to make a fuss. Samuel had questioned her strategy. He figured it would take a lot to distract parents from the return of a prodigal daughter, with her own daughter in tow. *Ach*, well. If needed, the fatted calf could conceivably be nearby.

Surely they would feel like celebrating? He didn't know Willa Lapp, and her husband not much better, but if Willa was anything like Hannah or Gail, she'd at least be reasonable, if not pleasant. As was Zebulun Lapp, Gail's *daed*. Reining Belle into the Lapps' lane, Samuel's stomach lurched at the possibility that Gail's family would give her a poor reception. If they did, it would be his fault for pushing her back into a situation she'd wanted to avoid. He admired her bravery in facing uncertain circumstances. Continuing up the lane, he slowed Belle to a walk. No truck, with or without a trailer, was in the farmyard. He'd arrived first. Or she wasn't coming.

If she didn't, it was no more than he deserved for tangling up her life. After securing the reins and setting the brake, Samuel sat for a moment, his mouth dry at fears for Lily that Gail had revealed yesterday.

As it was Visiting Sunday, he'd been out visiting. While doing so, he'd subtly asked around. Gail's fears had merit. Bishop Weaver's wife was a force to be reckoned with. With the authority of her husband that she used as a tool, few succeeded in disputes with her. As Amish, any disputes should be few and far between, but they were still people with human weaknesses. Samuel had been told of a disturbing number of situations where Bishop Weaver had subverted members' personal needs for the needs of the community. Needs of the community that seemed to benefit some—usually those close to the bishop—more than others.

If Gail lost Lily because of something

he'd inadvertently set in motion… Samuel clenched his hands. He didn't know what he'd do. He thought he'd been helping her reunite with a family she obviously missed and needed. Blowing out a tense breath, Samuel stepped from the buggy. He was getting ahead of himself. No use borrowing trouble. But if it came to that, he'd do everything in his power to prevent the situation. In the meantime, he was a horse trader, so he'd go inquire if a farmer was interested in a horse.

After tying Belle to the hitching post, Samuel entered the barn through the milk house. Whereas he only kept one cow for personal use and some surplus to sell, the Lapps milked several, selling the milk to the local cheese factory. Rows of clean milk cans lined the wall in preparation for use. The truck must've picked up today as there were no full cans cooling in the enclosure. Samuel carefully stepped across the pristinely scrubbed floor into the attached barn.

"Hallo?" Samuel lifted his voice to be heard in the cavernous structure. Visiting between farms was a common occurrence in the Amish community.

"Ja?" The response came from farther down a long alleyway. On his way to it, Samuel passed several stalls of Belgians, recently

fed. Although tempted to linger with the gentle giants, he recognized it as a delaying tactic and continued on until he stepped into the milking parlor.

Twelve black-and-white cows were in stanchions contentedly munching hay, six on one side of a center alley, six on the other. They paid him no attention, but the older man, older woman and teenage boy crouched beside the cows as they hand milked looked up as he came in.

"Samuel Schrock. *Wie bischt du?*"

"It's going well. I came to see how your family was doing." Despite his hearty greeting, Samuel's palms were sweaty. He slid them down his pants before he stepped farther into the alley.

"Bin gut." Zebulun Lapp responded without breaking rhythm on the hiss of milk filling the stainless-steel pail.

Samuel hoped it stayed that way when the man experienced the shock of a returning daughter and grandchild. "Saw Hannah the other day. She mentioned one of your horses was getting a bit long in the tooth." It was a bit of a stretch, but it provided him a reason for stopping by. "I was wondering if you might be in the market for another Standardbred and what you'd be looking for, so I could keep an eye out for it."

It was quiet except for the hissing of milk and a few stomps of the cows as Zebulun considered his question. Samuel took the moment to nod at Willa Lapp and one of Gail's younger *brieder*. It was when he'd really looked at Willa last Sunday at church that he'd known Gail was a missing part of the family. She was a brunette replica of her blonde *mamm*.

"*Ja.* I suppose it's time to think about using Daisy more for the shorter trips. What have you been seeing?"

I've been seeing members of your family and soon so will you if the childish voice I hear from the direction of the milk barn is who I think it is.

"This isn't Samuel's house. Why are we here, Mommy?" Lily chirped from the backseat as she looked out the window at the pristine farmyard.

That was a good question. Gail pressed a hand to her stomach as she unbuckled her seat belt. Why were they there? They almost weren't. Even now, parked in the yard, she considered starting up the truck again. But she didn't. She'd run away four years ago. And she was getting tired of running.

"Is this another Amiss place?"

Gail could hear Lily shifting in the back-seat. Any minute now she'd work her magic and be free of the car seat. Heart pounding in her throat, Gail opened the door and slid from the truck. At least Samuel was here as she'd requested. If she hadn't seen his mare tied to the hitching post, she might not have pulled in. But she was learning that, unlike a previous charming Amish man she'd known, Samuel was a man of his word.

When she opened the back door of the truck, Lily was slipping her arms from the straps. Gail reached in and lifted her down. "Yes, sweetie. This is another Amish place. This is the first Amish place Mommy ever saw." She inhaled deeply. "And we're going to go see some people Mommy knew a long time ago. Before you were born."

No one came out of the house, which was a relief. Just before they reached the door that Gail knew led to the milk barn, it swung open. Hannah stood at the opening, her smile as broad as the door she was standing in.

"I came out of the house when I saw Samuel go into the barn. I was hoping you'd come."

Tears welled in her blue eyes. *"Denki."* She stepped forward to engulf them both in a hug.

The tension around Gail's neck and shoulders loosened. Oh, she'd missed this. She'd missed family. She'd missed home. Maybe finally coming here was the right thing, after all. But what would it lead to?

"It smells funny in here. Why does it smell funny in here?"

The two sisters leaned back with watery chuckles at Lily's insistent questions. Lifting Lily into her arms, Gail stepped over the high threshold and into the dimmer light of the barn.

"There's lots of different smells in a barn, sweetie."

"Samuel's barn doesn't smell like this."

Gail had to admit that a milk house had its own unique aroma. "This room stores fresh milk, which does smell different when there's a lot of it together. Also, they work hard to keep this room very clean, so the milk stays clean. It's a mix of a lot of different smells rolled into one special smell."

Lily took an exaggerated sniff. "I don't like it. I like Samuel's barn better."

Hannah laughed. "It does take some getting used to." She let the door swing shut behind them. Her eyes met Gail's. The look in them told Gail that she could do this. Gail figured the message was sent because stark fear was probably reflected in hers.

They walked down the alleyway of the barn, with Lily commenting on everything. She wanted to stop and pet every horse they passed. Gail let Hannah respond to her daughter's chatter while keeping them moving.

As for herself, she was sensitive to the rattle of stanchions ahead, knowing that her folks were in the milk parlor a few yards away. Her stomach was sick with tension as she walked down the familiar passage. *Don't expect much. Even if they're glad to see you, Amish aren't physically demonstrative people. So if no one approaches, or gives you more than a nod, it's still good. If they reject you, or Lily, just say you were looking for Samuel about a transportation job. You can offhandedly apologize for the shame you brought upon them as you leave.* Although she knew an offhand apology would nowhere near absolve her of the guilt she felt for what she'd done and how she'd left.

So much for a quiet approach. Thanks to Lily's jabbering, when they stepped into the milk parlor, they had the full attention of everyone there.

Throat tight, Gail's glance swept the familiar scene. She'd come to the milk parlor since she was able to walk, probably earlier, before stopping abruptly four years ago. Ignoring the cows and surroundings, her gaze lingered on the people. She almost didn't recognize her *bruder*. Surely that wasn't Paul? Her heart swelled when she saw her *daed*. But it was the sight of her *mamm* that caused the tears to well in her eyes.

"Mommy, you're holding me too tight!"

Her mouth open and her face as white as the cow beside her, Willa Lapp lunged to her feet. She stood immobile for a moment before stumbling from the Holstein's side toward them, kicking over a full pail in the process. Just for an instant, Gail's gaze followed the milk as it poured down the gutter before she hastened toward her mother and was enfolded in a tight embrace.

Tears rolled down Gail's cheeks as she inhaled the fresh scent of her *mamm*'s dried-on-the-line dress that, up close, overruled the cattle aroma of the milking parlor. All too soon, her nose was stuffed from her crying. But it felt right when she felt her mother's tears against her neck, as well. She tightened her arm about her *mamm*'s lean, work-hardened frame.

"Too tight! Too tight!" Gail could feel Lily

wiggling between them. Sniffing, she leaned back and self-consciously swiped at her nose. Her tears continued to roll down her cheeks at the strong grip Willa Lapp had of her shoulders, like she was never going to let her go.

"You came back." It was barely a whisper. "Oh, I missed you so."

Gail nodded. "I am so, so sorry." Through blurred vision, she saw that her *daed* had stepped up beside her *mamm*. Placing a hand on her *mamm*'s back, he scrutinized Gail's face. After a moment a slight smile curved his lips. Knowing her taciturn father, for Gail, it was like the sun breaking through after a heavy thunderstorm.

"*Welkom* home, *dochder.*"

Tears sprang anew at the warm weight of her *daed*'s hand on her back.

"I knocked over the bucket." Her *mamm* sniffed self-consciously.

"*Ach*, Willa, no use crying over spilled milk."

After they all chuckled over the joke, her *mamm* reached up to gently touch Gail's face. "*Nee, nee*, there isn't. We're so glad you're back."

Gail swallowed. She couldn't tell them right now it was only temporary. "Me, too."

Willa turned her attention to Lily, who clung, round-eyed, to Gail. "And who is this?"

Gail inhaled a shuddering breath as she

tightened her arms protectively around Lily. "This is my *dochder*, Lily." Seeing nothing other than wonder in her parents' eyes, Gail continued hoarsely on the words she'd figured never to be able to say. "Lily, this is your *grossmammi* and *grossdaadi*."

Willa silently pressed her fingers to her mouth as she blinked back tears. Zebulun's hand moved up to tighten on his wife's shoulder. Gail could see her *bruder* Paul in the background, quietly nodding his head. What was he, fourteen now? Oh, he'd gotten so tall.

"Are these my Amiss, too?"

Gail bit her trembling lip before she could respond. "Yes, sweetie. These are your Amish, too. They're very special. This is Mommy's mommy and daddy."

"You wear a hat like Samuel. He let me wear his hat."

Gail caught her breath when her reserved father lifted his straw hat from his head, leaving an indented ring in his gray-brown bowl-cut hair. "Would you like to wear my hat?" With a smile and an eager nod, Lily slid down from Gail's arms and reached for it. "I like horses. Could you show me your big horses?"

Zebulun's mouth tipped up at the corners. "*Ja, ja*, I can do that." Careful to give the little girl space, he reached for his wife's hand.

"Come, *grossmammi*." Keeping one hand on the oversize hat to secure it to her head, Lily reached out with the other to grasp a few fingers of Zebulun's free hand. Gail heard her mother gasp softly at the action. The trio headed back toward the draft horses' stalls, Lily already chattering with excitement about the barn, cows and big, big horses. When they passed Hannah, standing at the end of the alley, she sent a grateful smile to Gail and turned to join them.

Gail watched the group pass the last stanchioned Holstein and leave the milking parlor. She'd never seen her parents stop in the middle of doing chores. Slack-jawed, she turned to find Samuel's eyes on her.

"Better go with them." He winked and nodded to the exit behind her. "They're new at this." He clamped his hand on Paul's shoulder. "I suppose that makes you an *onkel*. Better get in there in case they're setting up the rules of these new relationships."

Paul stepped forward without hesitation. Reaching out, he awkwardly patted Gail's shoulder as he passed. Gail lingered a moment longer, her gaze on Samuel. "Thank you," she mouthed, not even having any air in her tight chest to vocalize the words. "*Denki*. For giving me my family back."

"Go catch up," he encouraged. "Or they'll be so enthralled by Lily they won't even know you're here." With a wobbly smile, Gail hurried to join her family.

When they returned to the parlor later, after having met all the farm's horses, the chickens, the rest of the cows, the fattening hogs and the two Border collies, Samuel was finishing milking the last Holstein.

"Samuel Schrock, you didn't need to do that."

"*Ach*, no problem, Zebulun. I've milked a few cows before. And you were busy."

Nodding, Zebulun glanced at Gail and Lily before returning a speculative gaze at Samuel. One Samuel apparently read as well as Gail did.

"And speaking of milking, I have chores of my own." With a wave and a single nod himself, Samuel headed down the milking parlor toward the alleyway that led out of the barn, hesitating only briefly when Lily called out to him.

"Bye, my Amiss man!"

He turned to walk a few steps backward. "Bye, Lily." Then he was out of sight.

But not out of mind.

He'd made this possible. He'd done what Gail had thought impossible. She'd been reunited with her family. And it was *gut*. Very *gut*. For a moment longer her thought was on the man and not the family that now surrounded her. *Oh, Samuel. If she wasn't careful, a girl could so easily fall in love with you.*

Chapter Thirteen

The sun was already inching up the sky in front of them. It was a little later than normal when Gail picked Samuel up that Thursday. Extremely aware of his presence on the other side of the truck's worn seat, Gail wondered if the days since she'd last seen him had seemed as long to him as they had to her.

Sunday had been *wunderbar*. She and Lily had stayed long into the evening, past Lily's bedtime, in fact. Her other three brothers had returned from visiting friends and joined them. They laughed at supper, talking of things they'd done as a family when Gail was still there. When her *brieder* had teased Gail that she'd surely forgotten how to drive a horse and buggy, she'd reminded them that she drove more horsepower than they did every day.

Everyone had fawned over Lily. Gail figured her daughter had more piggyback rides with her new *onkels* than the drivers at the track had harness races during the season.

Although Willa Lapp had worn a smile all evening, Gail caught a few gazes where, although joy was at the forefront in her *mamm*'s eyes, apprehension framed the backdrop. Willa didn't look surprised when, at a quiet moment while doing dishes, Gail told her that their return wasn't the beginning of something permanent and added that the visit needed to be kept quiet. Although Gail didn't elaborate, it seemed her *mamm* had an inkling as to the reason why, when her gaze drifted to Lily, who was sitting on Hannah's lap, trying to darn her first sock.

It was a teary farewell when everyone followed them out to the truck to say goodbye. But Gail's heart was full that the whole thing had come about in the first place.

Because of the man beside her.

Thanks to him, her business had picked up, as well. Samuel's request to use her for his purchases at the auction barn had led to other jobs from there. In fact, if business stayed at this level through the fall, she'd be able to catch up on the truck and trailer payments. She'd received a letter from the bank, reminding her of missed payments and laying out consequences if she missed another. The additional revenue would definitely help in catching up. *Gott* was answering prayers she'd been too ashamed to voice.

And using a surprising person to do it.

While she'd enjoyed working with Elam Chupp, Samuel was proving much more dynamic with the Amish horse business. It was obvious he loved what he was doing. Just in the few hauls she'd already made related to the auction barn, she'd heard his name mentioned a few times. Always positively. Behind her sunglasses, Gail slid a glance over to her companion, taking in his broad shoulders under the black suspenders and his perfect profile under the flat-brimmed hat. Unseen was the surprising strength of character the attractive exterior contained. Gail hid a sigh in the wind rushing through the open window. She could understand. He was having a pretty positive impact on her, too.

Her attention focused on the four-lane highway in front of her, Gail debated dropping her right hand to drape it on the armrest between the seats. Just in case Samuel might notice and take it in his work-hardened one that rested close by. Her folks had held hands that night in the barn. The memory of that simple connection with another filled Gail with a contrary mix of joy and longing.

She was relaxing her grip on the steering wheel when she saw a vehicle approaching the upcoming rural intersection from the on-coming lanes. The green SUV didn't even pause as it turned left at the intersection. Pulling right in front of Gail, it straddled her two lanes.

The driver must have realized what they'd done. For a split second, the SUV hesitated. Gail knew in an instant they were going to collide.

Banging the horn, Gail slammed the brakes. Her heart froze at the sight of a child's face in the front passenger seat, directly in her path. She heard Samuel's sharp gasp just before the harsh squeal of the SUV tires ac-celerating joined the screech of the truck and trailer brakes.

It wasn't going to be enough. Aware the lane beside her was empty, Gail jerked the wheel, steering the truck to the left. Skid-ding through the lane, they barreled into the intersection.

Gail's knuckles were white on the wheel. The foot not on the brake was braced against the floorboard, her leg stiff as iron. There was a blur of red out the open window as they shot past the stop sign. With a jolt, the truck hit the curb that marked the edge of the intersection. The cab shuddered and a chilling rasp echoed through it as they bucked over the curb, the racket of the trailer lurching over behind them. Gail's seat belt tightened as she slid toward the door at the slant of the median they now bounced along. Only when the truck—slowed by tall grass and soft soil along with her braking—lumbered to a halt, did she draw a breath.

"Are you all right?" Her shaking voice matched the tremors that raged through her system. Contrarily, her body felt almost too stiff to move.

The airbags hadn't deployed. Steadying herself on the steering wheel, Gail turned to see Samuel and sagged with relief. His right hand on the handgrip by the door, the other braced on the dash, he looked tense but okay. "*Ja.* You?"

"*Ja.*" She echoed his response automatically. Heart pounding, she struggled to release her rigid grip of the steering wheel. "I need to check the SUV. I saw a child in the front window. I was afraid I'd hit them. I was afraid I couldn't avoid hitting them." Gail was babbling, but she couldn't stop.

"But you didn't. Praise *Gott.*" Unlike hers,

Samuel's hands were steady when he unbuckled first his seat belt and then hers. Flipping up the armrest between them, he slid down the slight decline caused by the truck's tilted position and pulled her into his arms. Gail didn't resist. She drew from his calm strength. A few moments passed while her tremors dissolved to sporadic shudders before she felt capable of pulling back.

Praise *Gott* indeed. For so many things. Praise Him that there wasn't anyone else at the intersection, that she'd known there was no one in the passing lane when the SUV pulled out. That there'd been no horses in the trailer, as they'd surely have been hurt.

They'd been blessed. Thank You, thank You, thank You, *Gott*. Now if only the other driver and child were safe, as well.

"I have to make sure they're all right."

"You okay getting out on that side?" At his question, they both looked out the windshield beyond the slanted dash. The incline the truck was parked on wasn't that steep. Not like fifty yards farther, where the median dropped into a deep ravine.

"I'll be okay." When she lifted the handle, the door swung hard and bounced on its hinges. Cautiously climbing out, Gail looked behind her to see the trailer jackknifed at an odd angle, tipped in the median so she could see the top of its sun-faded roof. Although her new tires seemed unaffected, at the front one's skewed appearance in the wheel well, Gail knew she wouldn't be as lucky with the axle. Her legs felt heavy as she waded through the knee-high vegetation and rounded the front of the pickup. The truck's grille had grass wedged in crevices and the front bumper tipped up like a curled lip, along with some other new scraps and dents. The aesthetic factors were the least of her worries. The truck wasn't going anywhere. Neither was her future at the moment. But more important now was the condition of the passengers in the green SUV parked on a subsidiary road.

Samuel joined her. Forcing a deep breath into still-tight lungs, Gail checked for traffic before crossing the pavement to the crossroad. The SUV's doors were open. A woman on a phone paced a continuous route between the two open doors on the driver's side.

"I pulled right out in front of the truck. I didn't even see it." The woman was talking in a high, rapid voice with someone. "Yes, yes, we're okay." The woman paused and propped herself against the open front door of the SUV. "We're all okay, but I'm still shaking." She turned toward Gail and Samuel's approach. "I have to go. The other driver is here. Yes…yes. I'm able to drive. I'll see you at home. I know. I love you, too." Beneath the woman's sunglasses, tears were streaming down her cheeks.

As she approached where the woman sagged against the door, Gail glanced into the open car. Her stomach lurched and she stumbled into Samuel, who caught her with a hand at her side. There was not only the child of around ten that she'd seen through the front window, but two smaller children in car seats in the back as well, one facing forward and one, still a baby, facing the back of the seat. The possibility that they might've all been injured had she not cleared the back of the SUV almost made Gail slump against the vehicle, as well.

Lifting her sunglasses to the top of her head, the woman straightened from the door. "Thank you. My husband owns a freight company and I—I know I'm not supposed to say anything that might admit guilt or something but…" She teared up again. "I can't thank you enough for missing my kids. I don't know what I would've done. I thought I'd looked but… Thank you." She sniffed loudly. "Are you okay?"

Gail could only nod. Her lips twisted at the question. Physically, yes, but not financially. "Are you? And the little ones?"

"Yes. Thanks to you." The woman looked over at Gail's rig, parked in the grass on the slanted side of the median. "How's your truck? And trailer? Any damage?"

Gail's gaze followed the woman's to where her now-broken financial future rested. "Yes, but I don't know the extent yet."

"I'll get you my contact number and insurance. Whatever's damaged, we'll get it fixed. Again, I can't thank you enough for missing my kids." Anything else the woman said was lost as she leaned into the SUV for the purse that rested on the console. While she was in there, the two older children chattered in high, excited voices.

Numbly, Gail turned and stared across the road to where Samuel had returned to the truck and trailer. The woman's insurance might cover the repairs, but how long would Gail be without them? She'd needed every job she could get to pay bills. Bile coated the back of her throat when she recalled how she'd been mentally paying bills with money she didn't have just a short time ago. Would she be able to recover from this loss of business while her rig was in the shop? Or get the jobs back that she'd lose in the meantime to someone else? Was the truck repairable?

Shakes now receded, Gail felt mentally and physically exhausted. Her breath left on a shuddering sigh. However she got home tonight, on the way there, she'd need to pick up a paper to check the help-wanted ads. The sooner she started on one, probably two, the better. Even then, her and Lily's financial outlook was dire.

But at the moment at least the children in the SUV were safe. She could live with that. As to the other, time would tell.

After she and the woman exchanged information, Gail crossed back to the median, where Samuel waited by the wheels of the trailer.

"I don't know," he responded to her questioning look. "On a buggy, I could see a problem. On this…" He shook his head. "Got some new dents, which probably isn't an issue for you, but something metallic smells hot, which probably is."

Gail mutely nodded. She'd smelled it, too. With unfeeling fingers, she punched in the phone number of the insurance company on her cell.

Hours later, hands braced on the counter of a repair shop that'd been recommended, Gail glanced at the clock. It seemed like forever but was only early afternoon when the repairman apologetically told her the bad news on the trailer. The truck was even worse and it would be late next week before parts were in and both were repaired. She'd told the shop to go ahead and fix it. She had no choice. Even if they were repossessed, they'd need to be repaired.

Mentally and physically sick, she stumbled from the counter to where Samuel stood at her approach in the small waiting area. "I'm so sorry. You wanted to go to the track. I can call and get someone else to take you. You might be able to salvage a bit of your trip."

"Don't worry about it. I've already had enough adventure today. I imagine that next week there'll still be a horse or two that has more of a future pulling a buggy than a racing bike." While she stuffed the paperwork into her purse, Gail felt his eyes on her. "What are you going to do?"

It was a good question. Gail really didn't know. First step would be to somehow get a ride. She needed to go home to Lily. She needed to hug her daughter. After that... She'd have no means of transportation in a small town. Not planning on using her high deductible insurance, she wasn't familiar with the options, and even less with the woman's insurance company.

Blinking back tears, Gail put a hand on her leg to stop its frenzied shaking.

"I'll call an *Englisch* driver. They can take us both back toward Miller's Creek."

"I couldn't let you do that," Gail automatically protested through numb lips.

"I'm going back anyway. I'm assuming you live somewhere in the same direction."

At the mention of Miller's Creek, the warm, comforting sensation of how she'd felt with her family washed through Gail. In its wake was emptiness at the thought of— with no transportation—being limited with Lily to their stark basement apartment. Yes, Miss Patty would welcome them to join her upstairs, but it would still be cramped for the three of them. In their small village, she'd be lucky to find any work. No buses ran in town. She couldn't reach another town without a vehicle. And they'd still have daily living expenses. With nothing to live on.

Gail closed her eyes, wishing for a place to just…be somewhat whole. When she opened them, Samuel was watching her. Even in the shade of his straw hat's brim, she could see the concern in his blue eyes. And she knew where she wanted to go.

"*Denki*. See if they would mind me picking up Lily before taking us to my folks' farm. I'll call the babysitter to let her know what's going on."

Samuel nodded solemnly, but Gail could tell he approved of her plans.

In a daze, Gail walked out of the repair shop and sat down on the curb to call Miss Patty. A week ago staying with her family would've been the furthest possibility in her mind. Now they were a sanctuary. But it could only be a temporary one. Her financial problems and the threat should a specific someone in the community learn of her daughter raged like dark thunderheads on the horizon.

Gail hoped she could weather the storm.

Chapter Fourteen

"You always go for the border pieces."

Hannah pressed a blue puzzle piece into place. One the color of Samuel's eyes, Gail couldn't help thinking. Pushing a flat-edged piece in her sister's direction, she chided herself to get him out of her mind, where he seemed to have become a permanent fixture.

"Maybe it's because I like clearly defined boundaries." Hannah matched the edges on another two puzzle pieces before discarding one. "Maybe it's because they're the easiest to find. Or…" She smiled sweetly at Gail while she leaned down to run a hand over the head of the black-and-white dog lying on the floor beside her. "Maybe it's because it's related to my dogs."

Gail giggled at the absurdity as she nudged pieces around with a finger, trying to sort them by color, her go-to when working on puzzles. She couldn't remember the last time she'd allowed something so foolish to make her laugh.

Despite everything, it had been a *gut* day. Gail blinked in surprise at how quickly she'd reverted to thinking in Amish terms.

Her family had been surprised and delighted yesterday afternoon when the *Englisch* driver had dropped Lily and her off. After ascertaining that Gail was physically all right from her frightening experience, the Lapps assured Gail that she and Lily were welcome to stay. Gail made a point to tell them that it would only be for a few days. She wondered later if that was more to remind herself.

Except for the attention that everyone paid to Lily, it'd been as if Gail had never left. Used to early mornings, she'd risen with the rest of the family and helped her *mamm* and Hannah with breakfast. When Hannah left for her job at the quilt shop in town, Gail assisted her *mamm* with laundry. Her *brieder* had taken Lily to the barn with them for chores. It was hard to tell who was more excited for the adventure, her *dochder* or the new *onkels*. Taking pity on her as she apparently remembered Gail's love for the live-stock, *Mamm* encouraged Gail to join them.

She'd relished all of it. The milking, the egg gathering, teasing her *brieder* during lunch-time, helping hitch up the Percherons to rake the mowed alfalfa and working with *Mamm* in the garden later in the afternoon with Lily hopping from plant to plant in wonder. Both she and Lily had flinched when their tender bare feet encountered rocks but being able to wiggle her toes in the tilled sun-warmed earth between the rows of vegetables had been worth it.

There were shadows over the visit, though. The first was why she and Lily were there.

After confirming her rig repair with the insurance company and the shop, Gail had turned her cell phone off, leaving it on the dresser of the bedroom she was sharing with Hannah and Lily. It saved the battery, as there was no way to charge it since the farm didn't have electricity. Shutting it down also severed, just briefly, her cares in the *Englisch* world. There was nothing she could do right now re-garding finances with no transportation.

While she'd determined the woman's insur-ance did cover rentals, it had a dollar limit. The size of the truck she'd need to pull a trailer would be out of the allowance range.

Before she'd shut the phone down, Gail had called her customers and told them she'd be unavailable for a while. She could only hope they'd still want her services when her rig was ready again. Following the last call, she'd sat on the bed in the quiet bedroom a moment until the nausea that churned in her stomach at her situation passed. Whether she lost some customers or not, and even with whatever part-time jobs she could pick up, she'd be late on another payment.

It took the reminder that *Gott* had taken care of her so far to get her off the bed. He said to be anxious for nothing and pray. He also said to consider the lilies that did not toil, but that Solomon in all his glory wasn't clothed, as well. Gail wasn't so much worried about clothing her own Lily. Keeping her fed and a roof over her head in the *Englisch* world and keeping custody of her *dochder* in the Amish one were what kept Gail up at night.

Which was the other shadow over their unanticipated stay.

Any buggy that went by or one that happened to turn into the lane was a risk that Ruby Weaver would find out Gail was back in the community. Back, unmarried and with a child of an age that could be connected to her involvement with the bishop's son. For the first few hours of the day, Gail had stiffened every time she'd heard a clip-clop of a horse going down the road.

But as the joy and comfort of having her family around her grew, her anxiety receded. Surely *Gott* wouldn't punish her that way for coming home? For this brief time with her family, Gail wanted to just…be. To recover some of the lighthearted girl she once was. To relax and enjoy what she and Lily might never have again. Surely *Gott* would allow that?

The silence in the gas-and lantern-lit room was broken when Dash, the male Border collie outside, barked. Woofing quietly, Socks got up from where she'd been curled at Hannah's feet and trotted over to the door. She woofed again, but her white-tipped tail wagged gently back and forth.

Gail glanced from the door to her *daed*, who was reading the Amish newspaper, *The Budget*, in his chair. She tensed; she couldn't help it. What if it was the bishop and his wife? Unclenching her fingers, she set a puzzle piece back on the table, glad that Lily, tired after an exciting day on the farm, was tucked up in a trundle bed upstairs.

Hannah calmly regarded her before selecting another flat-edged piece from those scattered in front of them. "Are you expecting company tonight, *Daed*?"

Zebulun Lapp looked toward the door over a drooping corner of his publication. *"Nee."*

With an unspoken glance at Gail, Hannah rose, crossed to the door and opened it.

When Samuel stepped through the door and bent to give Socks a pat, Gail exhaled softly in relief, her heartbeat accelerating. Firming her lips, she tried to keep a goofy smile off her face. After welcoming him in, Hannah returned to the table, leaving Samuel, hat in hand, to stand in the area between the kitchen and living room. His eyes widened when he saw Gail, making her realize this was the first time he'd seen her in Amish garb.

Zebulun let the paper sag a little farther as he regarded the new arrival. "I can only buy so many horses, Samuel Schrock."

To Gail's enchantment, Samuel flushed slightly. "I thought I might find out what Josiah was interested in. A young man wants his own rig when he comes into his *rumspringa*. I know Jonah already has one, but I've got a fast filly he might like to try."

"Jonah, Josiah and the two younger boys aren't here. They're at a baseball game."

Gail stifled a snort at the look her *daed* leveled over his reading glasses at Samuel. One that told their unexpected visitor that Samuel must've known very well there was a game and that was where most young men of the community would be.

Except, surprisingly, this one.

"*Ach*, I'm sorry I missed them. Perhaps I'll catch them at the barn-raising tomorrow."

"Perhaps you will. I'll tell them you stopped by." *Daed*'s gaze traveled from where Samuel stood to where Gail and Hannah were working on the puzzle at a side table. "In the meantime, I suppose, as you've traveled here for naught, one of my *dechder* could get you a glass of lemonade before you head back."

It was Gail's turn to flush, for when Samuel glanced toward the table, his eyes and smile settled only on her. "That would be much appreciated."

Gail bounced up, only because she couldn't sit still being the focus of his potent attention. "I'll get it. I'd like one, too," she chirped, conscious of Hannah's speculative smile. After retrieving two glasses from the cupboard, Gail pulled the pitcher of lemonade, ever present during the summer months, from the gas-powered refrigerator. She wasn't aware Hannah had moved from the table until she heard the slide of a chair on the linoleum behind her. Turning around, Gail found Hannah pulling a chair from the kitchen table over to the smaller one where they'd been working the puzzle.

"Have a seat." Nodding Samuel toward the third chair, Hannah settled back down in her own seat with a surprisingly sly look on her normally demure face.

Meeting his eyes, Gail handed the cool glass to Samuel. Her already rapid heartbeat escalated further when their fingers brushed in the exchange. Flustered, Gail scooted to the table, set down her own glass, slid into her chair and began sorting out all the pieces with flecks of red that she could find.

Samuel wandered over to the table and perused the thousand multicolored pieces scattered there. "What's it supposed to be?"

Hannah picked up the puzzle box cover propped against the wall beside her chair. The scene depicted a big red barn and milking shed with a stone foundation, ubiquitous to Wisconsin.

Samuel sat in the chair and eased it closer to the table. "You don't see enough of them in real life?"

"Not ones we get to put together."

"Anytime you want to crawl around on the rafters, let me know. I'll trade places with you."

Gail's hand jerked, knocking some puzzle pieces to the floor at the reminder of how Atlee had died, in a fall during a barn-raising. By the time she'd heard of his fate, she'd long realized that she no longer loved him. In fact, she'd doubted that she ever had. Only that she'd been mesmerized by his attentive charm. Still, Atlee was Lily's *vadder* and his death was a tragic loss for his family and the community.

Leaning down, she collected herself and the scattered pieces. What'd happened to Atlee hadn't been her fault. Regardless of what Ruby Weaver might do should she find out about Lily, Gail wasn't going to allow that to dim what had been a *wunderbar* day back with her family. And what might turn out to be an interesting evening as well, with their unexpected guest. Returning to the table, she found herself the focus of its two other occupants. Dropping the pieces from her hand onto its surface, she rummaged through the bright-colored assortment until she found a potential match and checked the fit. Although close, they didn't work together.

"We can't do that."

Gail saw Samuel's smirk from the corner of her eye as she searched for another piece. She continued, "Because there's no way the men would be able to fix the beef, potatoes and enough shoofly and lemon drop pies to feed the hundred or so women working on the barn."

Rather than become upset, Samuel's smile blossomed into his signature full-fledged grin. "*Ach*, I suppose we could feed you fried or poached eggs. Gideon and I have been practicing the many, many ways there are to fix eggs. There are a few I can't recommend. But I doubt it would be necessary as a hundred women couldn't raise a barn."

Gail nodded as if in thought and frowned. "You're right. I'm sorry, I was wrong."

"*Ja.*" Samuel's work-calloused fingers reached in to deftly pick up a piece and snap it in place. "I figured you'd discover that."

"It'd probably only take about eighty to get the job done."

Hannah's eyes were wide as she covered her mouth to smother a laugh. Gail's comeback had been a surprising statement for an Amish woman, but years making her own way in the *Englisch* world had made an impact on her. So had Samuel's presence. She felt lighthearted for the first time since she could remember. Lighthearted enough to flirt. Lighthearted enough to wonder if an attractive man's attention might be more than just a way of making conversation. She realized her world wouldn't topple over should she respond as an attracted young woman.

Because she was. Even if just for tonight it was safe to be so.

Samuel reached a hand over. For a moment Gail caught her breath, wondering if he was going to touch her. At the last second he dropped it to nudge a few puzzle pieces from the edge, back toward the center of the table. "Hmm. I might've had more luck playing baseball tonight."

"Do you play much?" From his physique, Gail figured he'd be very athletic on the ballfield.

"I'm usually very good at playing." Samuel took the puzzle piece she'd just set down and connected it with one of the stone foundation he was putting together before looking over at her. His expression told Gail he wasn't thinking of the same field she was.

A twinge reminded Gail that was what she feared with this man. He was exciting. He was attractive. But he was a much better player at this game than she was. And when she'd played before, she'd been the loser. Except for Lily. *But I'm wiser now.* Like the puzzle growing before them, she now knew the boundaries of where to stop the game. Didn't she? Gail looked into Samuel's smiling eyes. Suddenly dry-mouthed, she lifted her glass and took a hasty swallow of lemonade. Finding it much tarter than she'd expected, she started coughing.

"Are you all right, Abigail?" Hannah handed her a tissue for her watering eyes.

"*Ja*, Abigail. Are you all right?" Her given name on Samuel's lips sounded much different than when her *schweschder* said it.

Gail dabbed at her eyes. "*Ja, ja.* Too much, too fast." Like her attraction to Samuel. It was something she should take care to remember.

But that was difficult when sometime later he got up to leave. As twilight ran well into the evening and an Amish family's work began in the wee hours of the morning, Gail's *daed* had joined her *mamm* in retiring a while earlier. When Samuel stood, Hannah immediately got out of her chair, as well.

"Let me just clean up these glasses." She hurried them over to the sink.

Samuel looked at Gail. "Walk me out?"

Against her better judgment, Gail found herself nodding. A minute later she crossed the wide front porch and descended the steps, conscious of the man who walked a few inches from her. The hair on her forearm prickled. Crossing her arms in front of her to bring her senses back to good, predictable, unexcited behavior, Gail winced when she poked the tender flesh under her arm on one of the straight pins that held the front of her dress together.

"You all right?" Samuel opened the white wooden gate for her to pass through.

"*Ja.* Just scratched myself on a pin. I'd forgotten about that aspect of Amish life." Gail tipped her head back to take in the uncountable stars cast over the dark sky above. "Wow," she murmured. "I'd forgotten this aspect, as well. With no yard light, streetlight or anything to dim their glow, the stars are just…" Her voice drifted off.

Samuel looked up, as well. "*Ja.* Hard to find the words to describe it in any of the languages we speak, isn't it? It's like a window into heaven."

It was an apt description. Side by side they silently looked up at the multitude of stars that streamed into infinity above them. Gail felt small with the beauty of *Gott*'s creation and the fact that she had a place in His world.

From the corner of her eye, she could see Samuel's chest rise in slow, steady breaths as he took in the vast spill of stars. What would it be like to have this man in her world?

Although the flirty Samuel was stimulating and fun, it was this sensitive Samuel that was drawing her in. She could guard herself against flirty Samuel, having been inoculated by Atlee's more clumsy charms.

Gail was very afraid she could fall in love with sensitive Samuel.

She studied his profile in the muted light of the starry night. The shadows couldn't disguise the strength of his jawline or obscure his equally powerful shoulders. This was a man with whom one could take shelter from life's storms. Or if not shelter, at least he would stand strong alongside, come what might.

But his world was not her world. Gail stepped back while she still could. Samuel's horse shook its head, the bridle jingling against a background chorus of cicadas, chirping crickets and frogs from the nearby pond. Needing to break the magic of this unsettling man in the quietly settling evening, Gail strolled over to the front of the hitching post where his mare was tied.

Reaching out a hand, she smoothed the horse's forelock over the bridle. The bay raised her head and twitched her ears back, but otherwise didn't react to the attention. "Why do you call her Belle?" He'd told her once the mare's official track name had been Sour Grapes.

Samuel followed Gail over and considered his horse before turning and leaning his elbows back on the hitching post. "All females deserve to be considered beautiful. Some are beautiful because of their disposition, some in spite of it."

"What's Belle?"

Hooking a corner of his lips in a wry smile, Samuel tipped his head toward the mare. "She's an *in spite of.*"

Gail smiled herself and mirrored his pose against the cross rail. A squeaking of leather heralded Belle's movement behind them.

"When did you go from Abigail to Gail?"

She sighed at the question. "When I left home, I guess. It was bad enough that I looked and acted like a lost and overwhelmed Amish girl. I couldn't change those factors right away, but I could change where my name shouted Amish, as well."

"I like your name. Both of them. But *Abigail* isn't a name made for shouting. It's more one made for whispering. Softly." When Samuel shifted to face her, it seemed like the space between them shrank more than the physical inches of his movement. "Abigail."

The whisper of her name on the quiet night sounded like a caress. But she recognized the transition to flirty Samuel. "Does this work on Rebecca, Lydia and Rachel?" She whispered back names of girls she'd grown up with, women who could still be single in the community, for all she knew.

"Pretty much. Although I've not tried it on Rachel, as I think she's walking out with Benjamin Raber's older *bruder*, Aaron." He didn't seem bothered that Gail had called him out on his flirtation. Samuel's grin faded to a smile as he straightened from the hitching post to stand in front of her. "I do like the name *Abigail*, though. May I call you that?"

Gail pondered his request through several heartbeats as she recalled the difficult transition from one name to the other. Studying his shadowed face, she hoarsely responded, "I'm not sure I'm her anymore. Abigail was more naive. Trusting. She thought she was smarter than she actually was. Braver, until she found out she wasn't."

"I think she was very brave. I have a lot of respect for Abigail. But I have a lot of admiration for Gail." His words drifted to her in a murmur as softly as he'd said Abigail.

She was confused. Was this the flirty Samuel or the sensitive one? Before she could decide, an abrupt shove between her shoulder blades, accompanied by the jangle of Belle's bridle, sent her sailing forward into his arms.

"Are you okay?" It was surprising how gentle Samuel's strong hands were when they circled her upper arms and eased her away from where she'd sprawled against his chest.

"*Ja*. I can see now, though, why Belle's name is in spite of her disposition."

"Oh, I don't know. I think she's pretty likable right now." His hands now tenderly eased her closer as his head lowered.

Years ago young Abigail thought she'd learned something about kissing while foolishly enjoying the embraces of the charming Amish man she assumed she would marry. Older and wiser Gail acknowledged she knew nothing about it when this man softly kissed her lips. She'd expected a practiced flirt like Samuel to kiss as a way of taking. What surprised her was what he gave instead. Tenderness. Patience. Hope?

Her eyes opened when he ended the kiss. Self-conscious, Gail avoided meeting his gaze and glanced over his shoulder to see a shadow of a person in the lamplight in front of a second-story window. Although she knew it probably wasn't, in her bemusement, it seemed like someone was looking out at them. "It's like I'm sixteen again. Maybe I needed someone to keep a better eye on me then."

Samuel followed her gaze. "They care for

you." When his attention returned to her, Gail felt the weight of his pensive regard. "I think you're too hard on yourself. *Gott* is a forgiving *Gott*. Why are you so special that you don't think you can be forgiven for past mistakes?"

Was that why she'd left and stayed away? Running instead of returning? Because she couldn't forgive herself for her foolish mistake, and didn't think that *Gott* would, either? When did she become that person? Theirs was a community of forgiveness. Before she could wonder further, Samuel kissed her again and she could think no more.

A staccato sound drifted into her ears. Gail eased back, unsure if she was disappointed or relieved when Samuel let her go. She sagged against the rail. The clip-clop of hooves on blacktop carried through the cicadas' song that hummed through the farmyard.

"I better leave. That's probably your *brieder* coming home from the baseball game." Humor broke through the obvious reluctance in Samuel's voice. "As long as I don't actually talk with Josiah about a horse, I can come back to try again later." He leaned forward to kiss her on the forehead. His voice deepened. "Although we both know it's not him I'm coming to see."

Dazedly, Gail watched Samuel untie Belle

and agilely spring into the buggy before backing the mare away from the hitching post. Her gaze followed them down the lane before she was able to straighten from the rail. Regardless of her resolve, either sensitive or flirty, Samuel Schrock was dangerous to her equilibrium.

Samuel gave the buggy full of Lapp *brieder* a two-finger salute, but didn't stop when the young men called out a greeting. He let the mare set her own pace, smiling when he realized his heart was pumping faster than the tempo of Belle's quick trot. His matchmaking horse deserved whatever she wanted to do tonight. In fact, he might buy some of the premium feed in Miller's Creek and treat the mare. Watching the dark countryside sweep by, his smile expanded at the memory of Belle threatening the persistent Lydia with snapping teeth while nudging the reluctant Gail into his arms. Maybe he should let his Standardbred sort out the women for him.

Relaxing the reins in his lap, Samuel's smile faded. But he didn't want any other women. It was becoming more obvious to him every time he saw her that he just wanted Gail. Gail and Lily. They were a package deal.

The cadence of Belle's hooves on the road was

generally soothing music to his ears. Tonight it wasn't having the same mellowing effect.

Was he ready for fatherhood? Samuel always knew he was going to get married. While he certainly planned to have *kinder* in the future, he hadn't thought much of being a father. Now he did. Of being Lily's father. Gail's husband. Samuel inhaled a lungful of the night air as he realized how much he wanted to watch the inquisitive little girl grow up to be a young woman. His breath held in wonder at the thought of Lily as the eldest girl of a growing family, one with Gail as their *mamm* and him as *Daed*. Belle flicked her ears back in question at his long exhalation.

Ja, he was ready to be a husband. But was Gail ready to be a wife? An Amish wife? Her time in the Plain world was only a temporary one until her truck and trailer were fixed. She insisted her and Lily's future were in the *Englisch* world. Was Gail overreacting in her concern for Lily in regard to the Weavers?

Could he convince her to stay? Would it make a difference to Gail's fear of remaining in the Amish community, or her desire to stay in the *Englisch* one, if she was staying as a wife—*his* wife—instead of as a single mother?

Chapter Fifteen

"He likes you." Hannah's comment was quiet, as an exhausted Lily snored softly on the trundle bed in the upstairs room they were sharing.

The possibility sent a thrill through Gail. She concentrated on removing the straight pins that held the top of her dress together. "*Ja*, well. I'm sure he likes a lot of girls." To distract her sister, she added, "Tell me again why we use these things instead of buttons?"

"Because buttons are considered ostentatious and we aren't to wear anything that would make us *hochmut*." Already in her nightgown, Hannah removed her *kapp* and began taking down her hair. "And while, *ja*, Samuel flirts a lot, I haven't seen him look at other girls the way he looks at you."

Gail poked her finger in the process of putting the pins in the cushion for the night.

Frowning, she pressed the stinging pad against her teeth. *You deserve that for not paying attention. And it'll hurt much worse if you don't remain on guard against him.* Lifting her hands, she unpinned her *kapp*. Just for a moment she wanted to bask in the possibility that she could be special to him. *Bask quickly, though, because it won't last.*

She dropped the pincushion on the plain wooden dresser and glanced over at her sister. Gail couldn't help drawing a breath at the beautiful picture Hannah made with her golden hair streaming about her in the candlelight as she brushed it. Releasing a long sigh, she prepared for the inevitable. "What about you? Are you interested in him?"

Hannah's nimble fingers began the much-practiced task of braiding her hair for the night. "Samuel? *Ach, nee.* I'm cotton, plain and simple, where he's satin—smooth and probably a challenge to work with." She smiled at her quilting analogy. "He might have flashed his charm in my direction when he first arrived, but we both quickly realized we didn't suit. And since then, through Ruth, I'd like to think we've become good friends." Hannah cast a gently teasing glance at Gail. "But it wasn't a friend he was coming over to see tonight."

Nee. At least not according to what he'd said after he kissed her. Gail began taking down her own shorter hair, dropping pins to plink on the wooden floor as her shaking fingers fumbled in the task. Friends were all they could be. He was Amish. She was just wearing the trappings temporarily. She would be returning to the *Englisch* world as soon as her rig was fixed. Her only relationship with him would be a business one. Her stomach twisted at the thought that some morning she might pull into the yard to pick him up and a young wife would follow him out of the house to bid her new husband farewell for the day. Gail frowned. That was assuming her rig wasn't repossessed by that time, and she was still in business.

Needing to push the melancholy images from her mind, Gail sought a distraction. Hannah's comment reminded Gail of the many young men who'd flashed, if not their charms, then their attentions in her older sister's direction when Gail was around four years ago. After slipping out of her dress and into one of Hannah's nightgowns, Gail sat on the double bed next to her sister. "Why aren't you married? There were many that I remember who wanted to walk out with you. Surely there was someone who suited?"

Hannah's teasing smile faded. She looked down and secured the end of her braid. "There was one," she acknowledged softly. "But in the end, we didn't suit at all."

Gail probed for more information, but discovered that her gentle sister was more adept than even she was at deflecting questions about her past.

"I hope that you will rethink attending the barn-raising with us tomorrow. I think Lily would really enjoy it. The *kinder* have a *wunderbar* time playing together and the older girls do a *gut* job of watching over them while the adults are working." Hannah slipped under the cotton sheet, the only covering on the bed in the warm summer night. Tugging the edge from under Gail, she flipped it back, inviting her sister to do the same.

Gail froze at her sister's words. She couldn't go. Of course she couldn't. Ruby Weaver and the bishop would be there. The threat they posed to her *dochder* and their authority over those she loved in the community shouldn't be dismissed.

But Hannah was right on one thing. Lily would love it. In a childhood that'd involved responsibilities and chores from a young age, some of Gail's favorite memories of her youth were ones of playing with friends at work and social frolics. Her and Lily's current life left few options for her daughter to have playmates. But how could they add more? Perhaps find an *Englisch* church to join? For some reason, Gail couldn't get excited about the prospect.

"You know why I can't go."

"The community has grown since you left. There are a number of new families. New faces. Ruby spends little if any time with the unmarried *youngies* and no time with *kinder*. Even if she recognizes you, she'd have no reason to recognize Lily. With no *boppeli* pictures like the *Englisch*, it's unlikely that she'll recognize her son in your daughter."

Gail's heart pounded at the prospect. Would it really be possible? To be part of the Plain community again, even for a while? Perhaps for a long while?

Could she return to her family and way of life? Reaching out, she gripped the wooden headboard to contain herself before she leaped up in excitement. "I'll think about it," she murmured.

The risk would be great. But so would be the reward. What if Hannah was right? With their similar clothing and hairstyles, and never having seen her before, why would Ruby believe that Lily was Atlee's child? Gail snorted softly. Besides, if she were truly the jezebel that the bishop's wife had accused her of being, Lily could be anyone's daughter.

Gail slid under the sheet beside Hannah, prospects for the morrow racing through her mind. She adjusted the feather pillow under her head. If tomorrow worked for her and Lily living Amish, what about the next day, and the next? And if they returned to the Amish community, it would change the possibilities of a friendship—or more—with a certain Amish man.

Gail listened to the sound of cicadas and crickets that drifted through the open window. It was a long time before she fell asleep.

Samuel fished a few nails from the carpenter's apron at his waist while he slanted a glance at the man working on the next rafter over. Although they'd visited about farming and livestock after church Sundays and at auctions, he didn't know Jethro Weaver well. A few years older and married, he didn't attend the Sunday night singings where Samuel had gotten to know most of the unmarried men of Miller's Creek.

Placing one nail between his lips as he set the other, Samuel studied Jethro's profile as he secured a purlin board to the rafter. He wondered if Atlee had looked like his older *bruder*. Furrowing his brow, Samuel supposed the man could be considered handsome. The first nail slid deep into the rafter under the force of his hammer.

He plucked the second nail from his mouth, tasting a bitterness that had more to do with the thought of the man's *bruder* with a young, innocent Gail than the metallic flavor of the galvanized nail.

A clatter of boards disrupted the organized symphony of hammer strikes that filled the morning. At the sound of a shout, Samuel jerked his head up to see a trio of purlins tumbling down the rafter. Samuel dodged the falling lumber, but the boards struck Jethro Weaver, knocking the man off his precarious perch. With a startled gasp, he fell toward the empty space between the rafters.

Lunging forward, Samuel grabbed Jethro's scrabbling hand at the wrist. Both men grunted at the jerk and pull on their arms and shoulders when Jethro's dangling feet swung out over the unforgiving surface forty feet below. Samuel gritted his teeth against the strain on his healing back. His knees and feet scrambled for any anchor on the structure to keep from being pulled into the chasm.

A sharp-edged board gouged Samuel's

chest as he skidded forward a few inches, pulled by the man's hanging weight. His hat tumbled down past a white-faced Jethro. The man's eyes were wide with fear.

"I won't let go." The vow was to both of them. Samuel would either get Jethro up, or the bishop's son would take him down when he fell.

A sun-browned hand was thrust into Samuel's peripheral vision. Reaching down, it grasped Jethro under his opposing arm. A quick glance revealed a grim-faced Benjamin. Between the two of them, they lifted Jethro enough so he could get an elbow, then an armpit, over a board. From there, they worked until all three were perched, panting, on a secured purlin.

At the rattle on wood, Samuel shifted cautiously to see Malachi and Gideon scrambling their way toward him over the barn roof's limited surface. He shook his head and waved them back. When he went to rub his sore chest, he was surprised to find he still had his hammer clutched in a white-knuckle grip. Inhaling deeply to control his residual shudders, Samuel looked up to see horrified expressions on the two teenagers working farther up the slant.

As they looked as shaken as he felt, Samuel decided they didn't need further chastisement. Not too much anyway. Tapping his bare head, he advised them with a crooked smile, "You owe me a hat." Because his heart was still thundering, he added, "You knock us all off, it might mean more food for you at dinner, but it also means more work to do by yourself afterward. Have a care." The boys' jerky nods ensured there wouldn't be any more clumsy fingers for the rest of the day.

At the squeeze on his shoulder, Samuel gave a nod to Benjamin as his former co-worker maneuvered himself back to where he'd previously been working. Samuel glanced at Jethro Weaver. The man's face was still as white as his shirt.

To help him regain his composure, Samuel observed, "*Ach*, I hope I didn't swallow a nail. I'm surprised I didn't drop my hammer. Good thing, as the grip was only just getting comfortable in my hand." The man nodded solemnly, but some color began returning to his face.

"You all right?" Samuel asked quietly as the whacks of hammering, at first intermittently, then in chorus, began again around them.

With tight lips, Jethro gave a single nod and shifted back to the rafter he'd been working on. Samuel regarded his own rafter. Pulling a nail from his carpenter's apron, he positioned it against the raw lumber in front of him. He had to wait a moment for the tremors in his hand to stop before he could strike it with the hammer. Glancing over, Samuel found Jethro had set his hammer down and was just holding on to the board they sat on. It was a few moments before the man picked up his tool and continued his work.

Samuel blew out a breath between pursed lips. He knew he'd be shaken as well if he'd almost met the same fate as a deceased *bruder*. Setting the nail with a light tap, he frowned at the number of strikes it took him to bury it into the wood. Whatever he'd heard about the man's overbearing parents and dallying *bruder*, he'd gained respect for Jethro Weaver today.

Without turning his head, Samuel knew it was Gail's green sleeve that brushed his shoulder as she reached for his glass. Even after using homemade soap instead of whatever it was she generally used, he inhaled an essence of something that was just…her.

He'd wondered if she'd come. Knowing there wasn't any good way he could've asked Zebulun Lapp or his sons about Gail's plans, he'd kept watching for the Lapp women's arrival. A smile had lit his face when he saw Lily scramble from the buggy dressed in Amish clothing. While carpentry had been in the forefront of his mind, the back of it was wondering how Gail and Lily were doing. And why she'd decided to come. And if she was having any issues now that she was here.

Twisting slightly on the bench set up for mealtime, he watched her pour lemonade from a glass pitcher. *"Denki,"* he murmured and smiled. Nodding, Gail met his gaze from under her lashes, giving a private smile in return. Though the table where he sat with the other men was shaded by a huge oak, Samuel flushed. Swiveling back to his plate, he was conscious of Gail reaching on his other side for his neighbor's glass. He forked up a bite of food, but didn't identify the applesauce until his third chew.

Maybe the sun had affected him more since he'd lost his hat. Otherwise, why would one woman's small smile affect him so? In his peripheral vision, he watched her green arm appear and disappear down the line of men. Only when she moved to another table did he lift his attention to find Malachi watching him from over the planks that made up the makeshift table.

"Remind me not to work below you this afternoon. You're so distracted, I'm afraid you'll drop a hammer on me." After some initial chuckles, the men around them were quiet a moment, possibly recalling the tragedy that nearly occurred that morning.

Samuel cleared his throat. "*Ach*, if I did that, you know it'd be intentional."

"If you drop a hammer like you pitch a baseball, it'd miss anyway," Gideon joined in. The surrounding laughter came a little easier this time. "But you know, he hasn't been playing much baseball lately."

Accustomed to his *brieder*'s teasing, Samuel was surprised to feel his flush, instead of dissipating, creep farther down his neck. He missed his hat, wishing it was on so he could tug it down to shade his face. "I haven't had time, what with establishing a new business and doing the majority of the work at both farms."

"I thought you said he's been gone some evenings." Malachi took a bite of potatoes.

"He has. But not to play baseball. Because his glove still remains on the bench in the porch. And I haven't seen him at the games. I think he's playing at something else," Gideon mused. "In my experience, Samuel plays the field no matter what the sport."

"Besides the barn-raising, that was what brought me here today." Malachi stabbed a pickled beet. "I was hoping to see the woman who Ruth said Samuel was making a fool of himself over."

Samuel wished his normally reserved older *bruder* would just stay that way. Forcing a flippant smile, he retorted, "That's going a bit too far. *Woman* and *fool* are never used in the same sentence with me."

Deciding he'd had enough of his *brieder*'s comments, Samuel shoveled a few more quick bites from his plate into his mouth before standing and stepping back over the bench where he'd been seated. Studiously meandering over to where the empty plates were returned, he spoke a few words to men he passed on the way before taking a moment to chat with the ladies when he handed in his glass.

Looking in both directions to ensure that no one, particularly either of his brothers, was directly watching him, Samuel casually strolled over toward where Gail was now bringing desserts to cover a table set out for that purpose. When the other woman there left to get more plates, he stopped in front of the table. And in front of where Gail was passing.

"Anything you can recommend?" The question was pitched to be heard by others. When she stopped beside him, he murmured one that was not. "I'm glad you came. Are you doing all right?"

Reaching out a hand, Gail straightened a row of shoofly pie slices. "*Ja.* Those who have recognized me have been pleasant, as if I've never left. I hardly recognized Lily myself with her little *kapp.*" Gail looked over to where a group of children sat on the ground with their plates in their laps, supervised by a few older girls. She twisted her hands together. "I'm hoping others don't recognize her, as well. I spotted Ruby while we were setting up and have made sure that whatever she's doing, I'm doing something else. Hopefully she wouldn't even remember, much less recognize me, but just in case, I thought it wise to keep some space between us."

"Probably a *gut* idea."

Her gaze flicked past him to the rafters that stood out like a skeleton against the blue sky. "Be careful up there. I heard about this morning."

Samuel bit back the quip he would've used with anyone else. She had a reason to be worried. The thought that she might be worried about him warmed him. The possibility that she might be grieving for the father of her child, not so much. He wanted to ask which had prompted her, but saw Ruth coming with a tray of plated pieces of cake for the table. "I will be, don't worry."

He raised his voice. "As long as you're certain that Ruth didn't make the lemon drop pie, I'll take a slice of that, then."

"Samuel Schrock, you've made certain that you just 'drop by' at supper time so frequently that if my cooking hasn't sickened you by now, it's not going to." Ruth set the tray on the table and started unloading the plates of cake into empty spots. "Besides, I made a cake today. But I'm not going to tell you which one." Pivoting, she walked a few steps before saying over her shoulder, "I'll let you know when I'm out of range so you can start talking again."

Gail smiled, her gaze following the petite auburn-haired woman until she disappeared around a corner of the house. "I've always liked her."

"*Ach*, well, took me a bit, but she grows on you. Like mildew on a house."

Snorting, Gail lightly tapped him on his arm. "She's *wunderbar*, and you could've done a lot worse."

Samuel's thoughts weren't so much on his

wunderbar sister-in-law, but on how much he'd like to catch Gail's retreating hand and enfold it in his. "*Ja.* I suppose. She does me good by keeping Malachi out of my hair as she has him so busy on other things."

"You don't want a wife who's a driver?"

His gaze on the woman he'd met transporting horses, Samuel responded, "*Ja*, I suppose I could handle a wife who's a driver, as long as she's the right one."

Her blush contrasted sharply with the *kapp* she wore.

Looking over her shoulder, Samuel saw men were beginning to drift back to the barn. Dinner for them was over. Now was time for the women to eat before they cleaned up from the meal. "How long are you planning to stay?"

"We came in a couple of buggies. *Daed* said I could take Lily home in one whenever I needed."

Samuel would've said more, but among the exodus toward the barn were his brothers, who were giving him significant looks. A man peeled off from the group and headed hesitantly in their direction.

"Jethro Weaver," Samuel called cordially as the man approached. Gail immediately dipped her head and focused her attention on arranging the dessert plates on the table.

"*D-Denki*, S-Samuel." Jethro stammered over Samuel's last name, closing his eyes in obvious concentration before he could get it out. "S-Schrock."

Samuel had forgotten the man had a stutter. Now more aware of Jethro's overbearing parents, he wondered if that'd contributed to the impediment. The bishop's only son had a slight scar above his lip and furrowed lines in the brow above his guarded blue eyes. He reached out a hand, as calloused and work-scarred as Samuel's own.

Samuel took it and they shook. "*Schon gut.* You'd have done the same for me."

Jethro didn't say anything more. With a glance at Gail, he returned his attention to Samuel and nodded. When he left, Gail stopped shuffling the desserts and turned back to Samuel.

He sighed. "I suppose, much as I might hope, the barn won't build itself. I best be getting back to it." With a last smile for Gail, he reluctantly started toward the work site. His pace picked up after a few steps. The faster they got done, the sooner he could spend the evening not playing softball. As long as he kept his distance from Josiah Lapp today, he still had a reason to stop by their farm tonight on the premise of talking with the young man about a horse. Once there, maybe he could coax the man's sister out into the moonlight and ask if she'd like to spend her life with a horse trader.

Turning, he looked back to see if Gail was watching him, like he wanted to be watching her. His steps slowed when he saw the bishop and his wife standing in front of the table where he'd just been. Gail was nowhere in sight.

Chapter Sixteen

From his position up on the beam, Samuel could see a group of young children darting into the area between the construction and where the women were cleaning up from the meal. Knowing there were older children keeping charge of them, he wasn't worried. Amish *kinder* were accustomed to being at functions where men were working and knew to stay out of the way. He searched for Lily among them and smiled around the nail in his mouth when he spotted her dainty form. With her dress, miniature apron and blond hair under a diminutive *kapp*, she looked so Amish it was hard to envision her in the purple baseball cap and shorts she usually wore.

Setting the nail, he hammered it in. At a shriek from below, he glanced down to see an older Amish woman had waded into the group of children and grabbed Lily by the little girl's upper arm. Lily shrieked again and pulled back, but was no match for the woman.

The hammer was already on the beam and Samuel had begun his descent by the time the frightened wail "Mommy!" reached his ears. Splinters cut into his hands as he slid down the wood of the ladder, barely touching the rungs with his feet. Within scant heartbeats his boots thudded on the ground. A few ground-eating strides later, he swept Lily into his arms, breaking the black-clad woman's grip on the little girl's arm. With tears wetting his neck, Lily clung to him like a tickseed on socks.

Pivoting so he was between the girl and the rawboned, gray-haired woman who reached for her, Samuel stared into the face of Ruby Weaver. Although the color of her narrowed eyes was a faded blue, the look in them was pure steel as they matched his glare. Her lips pressed into a line as flat as the beams on the half-built barn.

"Who is that girl?" It was more of a growl than a question.

Samuel heard the percussion of running feet on grass before Gail skidded to a halt beside him, her face as pale as the cap on her head. Initially reaching for Lily, she seemed to think better of it when the little girl tightened her hold around Samuel's neck. Gail sidled closer to him, as well. Samuel longed to put his arm around her in dual protection and support, but knew that was impossible, even without the attention they were drawing from those nearby.

Her attention now focused on Gail, the older woman scrutinized her. "I remember you. You were the one provoking Atlee before he and Louisa were married. You were one of the Lapp girls. The one who left." Targeting Samuel again, Ruby tilted her head, trying to look around him to see Lily. Samuel adjusted his position so he blocked her view of the girl. Lily lifted her head and reached for her mother. Samuel tightened his grip. Without a murmur, Lily settled back in his arms.

"I asked you a question." The bishop's wife spoke again, in a tone that indicated she didn't usually have to repeat a request. "Who is that girl?"

Gail stiffened beside him. "That's my daughter."

Ruby shifted her penetrating gaze between Gail and the petite head pressed against Samuel's shoulder, darting him a suspicious look, as well.

"How old is she? And why is she blonde when you're dark?"

This time, when Lily reached for her mother, Samuel let her slide from his arms to Gail's eager ones. He figured both mother and daughter needed the contact.

"Ruby Weaver, if you know her, you know her sister. And her *mamm*. Both of whom are blonde."

"What do you have to do with this?"

Ach, she had him there. What did he really have to do with the pair beside him beyond realizing they were becoming more vital to his life than most anything else in it? Samuel crossed his arms in front of him. "I work with her in my horse-trading business."

The woman looked smug. From how easily the creases on her face fell into place, it was an expression she wore often. "Ah, *ja*, you took the business over from Elam Chupp. With my husband's support and approval."

Just in case Samuel forgot. And just in case he didn't know that Bishop Weaver discussed community things with his wife.

"*Ja*. It's been *wunderbar*. Thank you for asking. I don't suppose that you and the bishop would be in need of a new buggy horse? I've seen some fine ones. Ones that'd get you to church so fast your head would spin." The woman couldn't be charmed. Samuel didn't know why he wanted to poke at her like a boy who'd found a snake. Well, he did know. He wanted to take her attention from the two beside him. The two he wanted to protect, but had no right to.

"We're more than capable of getting anything that we might need." Ruby curled her lip.

"*Ja.* I heard that about you." Samuel felt the slight elbow poke of Gail, still standing tensely beside him. He knew he should back off, for as many reasons as boards on the barn beyond them, but he found himself rolling his weight forward on the soles of his work boots. This woman had been a factor that'd forced Gail from her home and into a four-year struggle by herself. She wasn't by herself any longer.

Before he could say anything more, a flash of dark purple materialized in his peripheral vision. Stiffly looking over, he saw his bantam-sized sister-in-law plant herself between Gail and Ruby Weaver.

"Abigail Lapp, I know you haven't done this for a while, but we haven't finished cleaning up. If you wanted a break, you should've said something. I know it'd be easier if we'd just use paper plates when feeding this many folks, but food always tastes better with real utensils and plates. Leaves us a lot of dishes. Which aren't done yet. So if you don't mind getting back to work…" With a hand on Gail's back, Ruth Schrock directed her toward the crowd of women who were watching from the area set up for washing dishes.

"I wasn't done with her yet."

Ruth glanced back over her shoulder. "*Ach*, neither am I, as the dishes won't wash themselves. Maybe you can catch up some other time, but not when there's work to be done." Ruth shot a look at Samuel. "Speaking of which, haven't you got somewhere else to be?" She jerked her head toward the unfinished barn.

Without another word, she accompanied Gail back toward the women, who parted like the Red Sea as they passed. Samuel watched until they stopped in front of the farthest wash station and Gail, obviously reluctant, let Lily down from her arms. The girl didn't stay on the ground for long, as Willa Lapp swept her up and settled her on her own hip as she manned a dish towel while Hannah slid in next to her and began drying plates.

Satisfied that Gail and Lily were safely surrounded, Samuel turned back to a frowning Ruby Weaver. The smile that always came naturally to him was forced. "I've been given my orders. I've got things to do." Heading toward the barn, he could feel the bishop's wife's attention—hotter than the summer sun—burning down his back.

Her ominous words rumbled after him. "So have I."

At the bell for an afternoon drink break, the men scrambled down from the barn like ants on a hill. As soon as Gail saw Samuel's feet hit the ground, she moved toward him, trying to make her purposeful direction look as nonchalant as possible. She paused to pour lemonade from the pitcher into a few glasses before she reached him, nodding at the men she vaguely remembered as she went. Lily was under the diligent care of her family.

She'd almost left, but Hannah, Ruth, Willa and some of their friends had formed a border around Gail and her daughter since the confrontation with Ruby. They'd kept Lily entertained by having her help with various small tasks. Gail's heart, the part that wasn't frozen with fear, had swelled with gratitude. She'd looked up from dishes occasionally and caught a few stares aimed in her direction from Ruby and her few confederates, but no one came near.

By the time she'd worked her way to Samuel, he was in conversation with Malachi and Gideon. He smiled at her approach. Gail couldn't help feeling warmed by the look in his eyes. When she filled a glass for Malachi and Gideon first, their smiles of thanks were edging closer to smirks.

"*Denki*, Abigail Lapp." Gideon nodded his appreciation for the refreshment. "Malachi, I talk with Samuel enough at home. I doubt he'll listen to me here any more than he does there, so I might as well go speak with Reuben Hershberger. Now that we have a few more draft horses, we can handle some bigger pieces of equipment."

"Don't feel bad, *bruder*. He never listened to me, either." Malachi shot an uncharacteristic wink at Gail. "Probably depends on the speaker. Anyway, I see Ruth trying to catch my eye. I'll see if she needs anything carried to the buggy while I'm down from the barn."

Samuel called after his departing older *bruder*. "She caught your eye a long time ago. It just took your feet a while to catch up."

Gideon snickered as he left. Malachi waved away the comment without turning. Gail found herself alone, facing Samuel. The blush that crept up her cheeks surprised her. "Drink?" she offered awkwardly.

Her blush spread at his smile. *"Denki."*

Pouring lemonade into the glass he held, her eyes widened at the smears of red on the damp surface. "What happened to your hand?"

When Samuel rolled his free hand palm up, she gasped. Samuel examined his hands as if he hadn't noticed the bloodstains and imbedded splinters there. *"Ach,* when I heard Lily's cry, I wanted to get to her as soon as possible. I guess the quickest route wasn't the friendliest."

"You're bleeding. Again." Gail set the now-empty pitcher on the grass beside them and reached for his hand. Holding it open, she gently touched one of the many splinters there. "I'm sorry you keep getting hurt protecting my daughter."

He shrugged. "She's worth it." He captured her gaze. "Are you all right?" The question was as soft as the look in his eyes.

Gail blew a stream of air through pursed lips. *"Ja.* I think so, at least." She lifted her free hand, which trembled slightly. "A bit shaken. I've been afraid of this for years. But you and Ruth deterred her. And now we have a human fortress surrounding us." Gail looked over her shoulder to find Lily assisting Hannah in providing drinks. "I'm amazed and humbled by how many friends I still have here, as if I'd never left. But Lily and I will go as soon as the drink break is over."

"It's *gut* having family close, *ja*?"

Gail turned back to find Samuel's gaze still on her. His look was intent enough that she knew it wasn't a simple question. Correction, the question was simple—the answer, not so much. But he was right. "It is. I only hope…" There was too much that she hoped for to say right here. The men were returning to their tasks. The exterior of the barn would be completed before nightfall. A few glances were thrown their way. Suddenly self-conscious, Gail let go of Samuel's hand. "If you can wait just a moment, I'll get something to clean your hands up a bit before you go back to work."

"I reckon I can do that."

Gail whirled toward where the women had been advised a first-aid kit was kept in the house.

"Gail." She turned back to see Samuel's hooked grin. He nodded to the pitcher at his feet. Returning with a grunt, Gail picked it up and hastened toward the makeshift table where she left the jug before rounding the corner of the house to enter the utility room door for the first-aid kit. Having located the white plastic box, she hurried out the door, directly into the path of Ruby Weaver and her husband, the bishop.

Her heart slammed in her chest as hard as the screen door that hit her in the back. After a stricken glance at their stern faces, Gail's gaze darted over the deserted area around her. A side yard with a few shade trees and a clothesline, it was on the opposite side of the house from where the day's activity was centered. She was alone. Ruby Weaver had chosen her ambush well.

"Abigail Lapp." Bishop Weaver's voice didn't invite any response. "I am told that you have a child. A child who is Amish."

Her eyes wide, Gail pressed her lips together, clutching the first-aid box against her churning stomach.

"An Amish child needs to be raised in the Amish community. Not an *Englisch* one. An Amish child needs to be raised by two parents, not by a woman without a husband," he admonished.

"She's *my* daughter." Gail could hardly get the words out.

"She is Amish and needs to live that way. An individual must be prepared to sacrifice for what is best for the community. We have a husband and wife in the community who are childless. They will be *gut* parents for the girl, raising her in the Amish way of life. I will speak with the ministers and deacons. You will be advised when the exchange is arranged." Matter obviously settled, he pivoted and left without a backward glance. Ruby Weaver gave Gail a smug smile before she spun and followed her husband.

Gail staggered to the base of an oak that shaded the side yard. Bracing a hand on its rough bark, she got sick. She'd forgotten the kit she grasped until she raised that hand to wipe her sweating face and the plastic grazed her cheek. Tossing it aside, she numbly heard it bounce across the grass.

"Gail, I need to get back up on the barn." Samuel came around the corner of the house. "My hands will be fine until…" He halted abruptly at the sight of her.

Sick with fear and guilt, Gail found a convenient target for her turbulent emotions that boiled over as anger like water out of an unwatched pot. He was responsible for this. Her attraction to him was what'd gotten her in this situation. Her penalty for wanting this man was losing her daughter.

"Stay away from me! If I lose her, it's your fault. I was just beginning to trust you! If you hadn't ambushed me by setting up a meeting with Hannah, this never would've happened! I should never have listened to… This is what I was afraid of all along. Why couldn't you just have left me alone? I might not have been happy, but at least I had my daughter." Gail panted, tears streaming down her cheeks.

"Gail, what are you talking about?" Samuel strode a few steps closer.

Pushing away from the oak, Gail held out a hand to ward him off. She staggered when her knees almost gave out. "Bishop Weaver is taking away my baby."

Samuel's face went as white as the house beside him. *"Nee."* He rushed nearer.

Gail sliced her hand between them in a chopping motion. "And it's all because of you."

"Gail, we can sort this out. Nobody's going to take Lily from you. I'll do whatever I can to stop them. Please listen to me. We can…"

"No. You've done enough." Each word was punctuated by a hitch in her breathing. "Stay away from me. Why didn't anyone listen to what I thought was best? It was hard, but we were fine. We were going to be fine." Through tear-blurred eyes, Gail caught a flash of dark color. Clearing her vision with a swipe of the back of her hand, she saw that Hannah had rounded the corner. Her sister shot a stunned look at Gail, before shifting it to Samuel in question. He shook his head.

Skirting Samuel in a wide circle, Gail stumbled to her sister. "We have to go. I have to find Lily and we have to go. Please help me find Lily."

"Lily's all right. She's with *Mamm*." Hannah draped her arm around Gail. Instead of leading her back around the house where crowds of people were gathered, she opened the door to the utility room and shepherded her sister inside.

Once there, Hannah released Gail to lean her against the washing machine. She opened the door to the kitchen and, just for a moment, Gail could hear the hum of women chatting while they worked before Hannah slipped through and closed it behind her. Moments later she returned with a glass of tea and wrapped Gail's shaking hands around it.

"Now, tell me what's going on."

The tea jostled in the glass, but Gail was gathering control of herself. Hannah's face grew increasingly pale as Gail relayed what Bishop Weaver had said. Knowing Gail's involvement with Atlee years before, she didn't ask any questions.

"I'll get Lily. You head to the buggy. I'll meet you there."

Gail nodded. "I'll stay at the farm until *Mamm* and *Daed* get home so I can say good-bye this time."

Hannah's blue eyes glistened with tears before she blinked them back. "I'll tell them we'll see you there. What are you going to do?"

Gail set the glass down on the washer and rubbed a hand across her mouth. Her lips were so numb from crying she didn't even feel them. "I don't know yet."

"I heard some of what you said before I came around the corner. I'm sure Samuel didn't mean for this to happen."

Just when she thought she was back under control, Gail had to draw in another shuddering breath before she could speak. "This wouldn't have happened if he hadn't interfered. I don't know what I'm going to do if I lose my daughter, Hannah. I have been trying so hard for so long just to keep her."

Hannah pulled Gail into her arms. "I know. We have to trust *Gott*. He knows your despair and your love for your daughter. He will not forsake you."

Gail nodded against her sister's shoulder and gave her a last squeeze before stepping back. "I'll meet you at the buggy."

Hannah slipped out the door to the side

yard. Gail watched her sister go before she, too, left the utility room. As she gently pulled the door closed behind her, she realized it was like her life. A door she'd been hopeful and yet afraid to open had been flung wide. The glimpse inside had been tantalizing, but now it was slammed shut. Now she just hoped they could get back to what they'd been living without it being irrevocably changed, as well.

It wasn't to be.

Even as she and Hannah hurriedly hitched the family's old mare to the buggy, Gail could see the bishop and his wife, dragging an obviously reluctant Louisa Weaver behind them, snaking their way through the checkerboard of parked buggies toward them.

Gail's fingers strangled the breeching strap in her hands. "Get Lily out of sight."

Hannah wasted no time hustling the tired little girl into the back of the buggy while Gail hastily finished hitching up the mare. Burned out of all other emotion, only fierce determination fueled Gail as she braced a hand on the horse and harness to work her way forward to face the approaching trio. She shot a glance behind them to the nearly roofed barn. *Oh, Samuel. I'm so sorry. I wish you were here. I need your strength and support.*

"Abigail Lapp." The bishop's voice rang

out like he was addressing the congregation on Sunday. "You were going to run with the child. Back to the *Englisch*."

Gail pressed her lips together. She couldn't deny it.

"We brought Louisa to take the girl, as we feared you would do so. Louisa and her husband will give the child a *gut* home. Bring the girl out now."

"No." Gail crossed her arms tightly over her chest to hold herself together. A quick glance at Louisa revealed the frail woman was shaking almost as much as Gail was.

"You," Ruby spit, joining the fray. "You lured my son into sin. I'll not have my *kinskind* raised by such a jezebel." She tried to look inside the shadowed buggy. Not seeing Lily, she stepped around Gail to stride closer.

Gail shifted to block her. "I was wrong to do what I did with Atlee, but you will not take my child."

"It's what is for the best of the community."

"It's what is for the best for you." Gail's heart was pounding as she stared the woman down.

"N-nee!" Both women jerked at a nearby shout. Jethro Weaver was winding his way through the buggies at a jog. Gail initially thought his stammer was due to exertion until

she recalled his stammer earlier with Samuel. "S-s-stop this now!" He jolted to a halt between his mother and father. "You w-will not t-take someone else's ch-child."

Ruby narrowed her eyes at her only son. "You stay out of this. The girl is Atlee's. You and Louisa will raise her."

"*N-nee.* I w-will decide what h-happens in my own household." Jethro strode over to grasp his wife's limp hand. "Louisa is w-with ch-child." Both of them were red-faced. Gail was too stunned to care if it was due to embarrassment at the announcement or the situation.

A change came over Ruby at the disclosure. For a moment a wistful look was evident in her pale blue eyes. But it was for just a moment. Quickly her face tightened again. "But Atlee's child…"

"You w-will be glad about m-my ch-child." Jethro's throat worked as he swallowed. Briefly breaking his mother's stare, he glanced at Gail. "Go."

Gail didn't need to be told twice. She hurriedly climbed into the buggy.

"We will talk further of this." Ruby marched over to stand next to her husband, confronting the younger couple.

"*Ja*, we w-will, but n-not n-now." Jethro

loosely put his arm around his wife's shoulders and turned her in the direction of the distant barn. After a look back at Gail, the bishop followed after them.

Ruby stood immobile, staring into the depths of the buggy as Gail released the brake. "That is Atlee's child. She'll not be raised by a single jezebel in this community." Her glare returned to pin Gail in place. "Your…friend is still somewhat new in this community. His horse business depends on my husband's goodwill. Goodwill that would quickly fade should he be associated with such a hussy." The curl of Ruby's thin lips warned Gail that, should she remain, the bishop's wife would find a way to punish them for it. She, Lily and Samuel would all pay the price.

Shaking so violently she was surprised she was able to stay on the seat, Gail maneuvered the horse around the other buggies and headed toward the farm as fast as the mare could go.

Chapter Seventeen

The reins were slick in Samuel's sweaty hands as he guided Belle up the lane to his *bruder*'s farm. It was Thursday. He was hoping Malachi was at home instead of in town at his furniture business. As Samuel stepped down from the buggy, Ruth poked her head out the kitchen door and pointed toward the woodworking shop he'd helped Malachi convert for Ruth from one of the unused outbuildings on their farm.

When Samuel nodded and waved back, she disappeared again. Hands on hips, he took in the neat farmyard, although his thoughts were far from there. It'd been almost a week since Gail left the barn-raising and, from what he understood from Hannah, the community. When he thought they'd both had time to calm down, he'd called her. She hadn't answered and hadn't called back. After what she'd said…

Their last conversation had replayed in his mind over and over again. She'd been right. It'd been obvious from the start that she'd wanted to keep her distance. From him. From Amish. But he'd taken it as a challenge to his much-touted charms and pursued her anyway. And then… And then he'd fallen in love with her. With them both.

Picking up a small rock from the gravel under his feet, Samuel threw it. Belle jerked her head up as it clattered against the barn. Yes, he'd manipulated Gail. He'd set up the intentional meeting between her and Hannah originally because he was growing interested in his *Englisch* driver and he wanted any excuse to see her more. It'd also been an initial attempt to see if he could begin to crumble the Amish-to-*Englisch* barrier between them. Because of what he wanted. Not paying any mind to what Gail wanted. And look where it got her.

He certainly couldn't do what he really wanted anymore, which was to marry her. So if he couldn't do that, well, at least he could do this.

Ducking his head in the doorway, Samuel blinked a few times to adjust to the dimmer

room after the glare of the summer midday
sun. Inhaling the familiar scent of cut lumber and whiff of stain, Samuel glanced up to
see dust motes floating in the sunlight that
streamed through the skylights and high windows at the end of the building. A quick scan
of the neatly ordered room found Malachi sitting on a stool at the workbench along a wall.
His older brother looked up from where he
deftly worked a sanding block on the flat side
of an oak board.

Samuel sighed in resolve as he strolled toward where Malachi was working. "Smells
better than when it was a hog house. Looks
better than the last time I was in here, as
well."

Malachi grunted, but didn't stop his practiced strokes over the board as he watched
his brother's approach. Samuel's gaze drifted
over other pieces of oak neatly stacked on the
bench. "A cradle?"

Malachi hesitated before nodding with a
sheepish smile. Samuel hid his own grin at
the flush of red that edged up his *bruder*'s
neck. He was thrilled for his older brother.

"As particular as she is, I'm surprised she
didn't make her own." Ruth was an excep-
tional woodworker. Samuel respected her
standards, but not the few times early in their

relationship that she'd called him out when he hadn't matched them.

Malachi's smile expanded. "*Ja*. I had to convince her that I like doing things for her." His gaze dropped to the shaped oak in his hands. "And the *boppeli*."

"*Ja*." Samuel agreed faintly, but his hand clenched into a fist. He wanted to do things for the woman he loved.

But for him, the doing of things would be far easier than any convincing. After their last conversation, he didn't think convincing was at all possible. Reaching out a hand, he stroked it over the top piece of oak in the stack. It was smooth as glass under his fingers.

"I imagine a *boppeli* will change a few things in your life." Samuel strove to act disinterested as he lifted and examined some of the cradle components. "Will Ruth finally stop working when the *boppeli* arrives?"

Malachi tipped his head as he considered the possibility with his always busy wife. "I'm thinking it will slow her down some."

"*Ja*. I figured you might be busier, as well." Samuel closed his eyes as his pulse accelerated. This was what he came for. Might as well get it out there. As soon as he could swallow past the lump in his throat.

"Busy enough to need another worker at the shop?" Attention fixed on the oak in his hand, Samuel heard the rhythmic strokes of the sand block abruptly halt. He felt Malachi's sharp gaze on him. He waited until he heard the block slide again across the wooden surface before he turned to his *bruder*.

Although his hands had resumed their task, Malachi's eyes were still on Samuel.

"Part-time?"

The lump wouldn't go away. Samuel swallowed again. "Full-time."

Malachi's brow furrowed between his thoughtful eyes. "Even when you were a *kind*, you always talked about having a horse business. I thought it was what you always wanted."

Samuel twisted his lips at the brief realization and abrupt loss of his dream. "Now I want something else."

"Something? Or some*one*?"

Inhaling sharply, Samuel conceded, "I don't think I'll get the someone, but the something is helping her get what she wants."

"And you think this is it?"

"She needs money. More than she can earn. *Ja*, I love horse-trading, but it doesn't make much money. Sure, it's enough for me to live on here, but not enough for what she needs to keep Lily in the *Englisch* world."

"You think she'll accept it from you?"

"What's with all the questions? Are you willing to give me a job or not?" This was hard enough as it was without the soul-searching grilling from his brother. It wasn't as if he hadn't asked himself the same questions. And hadn't liked the answers.

"I think I'd be surprised if the woman who I observed would be willing to take money from anyone."

Samuel shifted to stare blindly at the wood-working equipment in the compact room. "I'd figure out a way to make sure she gets it."

"You already quit the horse-trading business?"

"I put out word at the track that I wouldn't be coming anymore and was looking for someone else to do it." Samuel faced Malachi again and spoke through clenched teeth. "So do you have a place for me at Schrock Brothers' or not?"

Setting his work on the bench, Malachi rubbed a hand across the back of his neck. "I'm already getting one new mouth to feed. If you don't find work, you'll be at my door making another."

Samuel knew his brother was teasing, but

he wasn't in the mood to joke back. "You don't have to worry about that. Somehow, I'll make my own way."

"*Ach*, that's not what I mean and you know it. Of course there's always work for you in the business." Shaking his head, Malachi stood from the stool and clapped a hand on Samuel's shoulder. "What happened? I remember a time when you told me that when you found the woman you wanted to marry, you were going to make it less complicated than my courting of Ruth."

For some reason the warm grip of his *bruder*'s hand allowed Samuel to relax for what felt like the first time since Gail told him that she never wanted to see him again. "If that's what you called courting, you needed some advice." Samuel put his hand up to rest it on Malachi's calloused one a moment before dropping it back to his side. "At the time it looked a little easier from my angle. Had I known then what I know now, I might've been a little more sympathetic to your plight."

"*Bruder*, I know you, and I have more confidence than you that *Gott* will help you through this. You've skated through your relationships with women, relying on your charm. Mayhap this time you need to rely more on Him." Malachi tightened his grip on

Samuel's shoulder briefly before letting go. "But you're not getting out of doing most of the farmwork."

Samuel nodded, recognizing his *bruder*'s comment as an effort to make him feel better. With a halfhearted retort, "Only because I do it better than you or Gideon," he headed for the door, his heart aching with equal parts relief and regret. He might not be able to be with Gail and Lily, but at least he could help them stay together and survive in the *Englisch* world.

Ducking out the low doorway, Samuel lowered his eyelids against the bright glare of the afternoon after the dimmer interior of the converted workshop. Hand on the rough boards of the doorjamb, he kept them down as he mouthed a prayer. *If she could find a way to forgive me,* Gott. He squeezed his eyes shut. He had no right to ask, but he added the words anyway. *And if You could help them find their way back home.*

Gail pushed the bank's recent letter and the calculator aside. She could punch all the numbers on it she wanted, but they wouldn't change the outcome. Even if all her customers returned after her absence, with or without Samuel's—her hand clenched on the pen she held—business, she'd lose the truck and trailer.

She'd made frantic calculations with numbers that were more wishes than realities—more part-time jobs, a full-time one, what she could get with her education and experience anyway—and came up with the same results. She loved her daughter, but love alone couldn't put a roof over Lily's head or feed her, something Gail could barely do now, much less pay any kind of childcare. There'd be no time or money to treat her daughter to any kind of life. And they'd always be only one step from disaster.

The pen rolled across the table's chipped Formica surface as Gail put her head in her hands. According to what the repair shop had said on the day of the accident, her rig would be ready tomorrow. With no way to do business, she hadn't needed the phone. Since she paid by the minute used, she'd kept it off. Numbly, she reached over to power it up.

Although it twisted her heart to consider it, maybe Lily would be better off in the Amish community with a two-parent family. In contrast to the bishop and his wife, Jethro Weaver seemed a decent man. Food and housing for her daughter would be no issue. She'd also have friends to play with. Community. And now a younger sibling. One parent would always be around, as an Amish wife's primary role was to run the home and family.

Gail's eyes welled with tears when she realized her parents could then see Lily. Maybe from a distance, at church and frolics. Maybe closer, depending on what could be worked out with the family Lily lived with. But at least they would see her.

But Gail would not. She couldn't stay in the Amish community and not be with her daughter.

Rasping in a breath, Gail's shoulders shook with suppressed sobs. She started at the touch of a hand on her arm.

"What's wrong, Mommy?"

Gail slowly sat up to find Lily watching her somberly. Snagging a tissue from a box on the table, Gail wiped her eyes and nose before opening her arms to draw her daughter into her lap. "Sometimes mommies get sad."

"Do you miss your Amiss family?"

Gail reached for another tissue. "I do, sweetie." After dabbing her eyes again and taking a few shaky breaths, she cuddled Lily against her chest. "What would you think about living with the Amish?"

"Would we have horses? And ride in a buggy again?"

Gail almost smiled at her daughter's first thoughts of a changed world. "Yes, but it would mean giving up TV and cartoons."

Lily was quiet a moment. "Would I see my *gr-grossmammi* and *daadi*? And Hannah and my *onkels*?" She stumbled only barely over the unfamiliar words.

Gail pressed a fist against her lips to quell their trembling before she kissed the blond head nestled under her chin. "You might see them, but you wouldn't be staying with them."

"Would I see my Amiss man?"

Gail's hand tightened, wadding the tissues in it into a tight ball. Oh, how she longed to see Samuel. To apologize for how out of control she'd been that day. Yes, he'd arranged things without asking, but the fault for Saturday's situation wasn't his. She was the one who'd ultimately decided to meet with her family. And she was the one who'd decided to go that awful day. The fault had been all hers. A tear ran a hot track down her nose to drop onto Lily's hair. "You might. I don't know."

Lily's little chest rose on a sigh. "I miss my Amiss man."

Gail's voice wobbled as she responded. "I know, sweetie. I do, too."

The perfect situation would've been to marry Samuel. Ruby could hardly argue against a biological mother in a two-parent family, no matter what she tried to stir up. Gail and Lily could return.

And Gail could be with the man she now knew she loved with all her heart.

She'd tumbled the rest of the way for him that day. Before that last, awful confrontation. It'd been a hard fall. Maybe that'd contributed to her overemotional reaction. Sensitive Samuel had pulled her in, charming Samuel had tightened the knot and protective Samuel had sealed the deal. For a while, when she'd thought there was a chance things could work out, that she and Lily could stay in the community, Gail had been counting the minutes until that evening, hoping Samuel would stop by the farm and she could give him a hint of how she'd felt.

Instead, she'd shrilled at him like a banshee and told him to leave them alone. Samuel probably never wanted to see her again. Gail couldn't blame him. *If this is the way you treat someone you love, he's better off without you.* With the wadded tissues in her hand, she dabbed at a fresh trickle of tears.

At the harsh vibration of the phone on the table, both Gail and Lily jumped. Gail reached over to turn the device toward her and saw a number she didn't recognize. Surely the bank wouldn't be calling so soon after sending the letter? Or was it the number of the communal Amish phone hut? Were the Weavers calling about Lily? Was it Hannah with news of her family? Hesitantly, Gail picked up the phone.

"Hello?" she answered dubiously. She cleared her throat. "Yes, this is Abigail Lapp." As Gail listened to the masculine voice on the phone, her tear-swollen eyes widened. Clutching Lily to her, she stood.

Chapter Eighteen

As the weight of financial worries had always hung over her during the time she'd worked at the track, Gail was surprised at the melancholy that washed through her as she pulled into the back parking lot Saturday for probably the last time. Turning off the key, she sat for a moment, listening to the transition from the rumble of the motor to the ticking of the cooling engine. The track and the truck had been good to her, in their own ways. Without them, she'd never have had this new opportunity.

You never know where *Gott*'s path will lead.

Without the wreck, a situation that had prompted despair, she'd never have connected with the owner of the freight company. The owner who was so grateful and impressed Gail had avoided a collision with his wife and children that he'd been trying to contact her for a week to offer her a job driving for his outfit. He was providing the vehicle and a salary that she and Lily could easily live on.

But they would be moving to another state.

She still hadn't heard from the Weavers. Maybe Jethro had been successful in his intercession? For his sake and hers, she hoped so. She prayed so. At least, that might keep Ruby's malice from being directed at Samuel.

The truck's door creaked as she pushed it open and climbed out. Upon locking it, Gail paused a moment to gently pat Bonnie's bug-splattered external mirror. Determinedly dry-eyed, she headed to the stables to find George Hayes. This new job and move should be the answers to her prayers. Her financial worries were over. But if that was the case, why wasn't she happier about it? Gail forced a semblance of a smile when she finally found George leaning against the fence as he watched his equine charges in time trials on the track.

His weathered face creased in a pleased greeting as she approached. "Gail! It's good to see you again. I'm assuming your rig is fixed and ready to go?"

Nodding weakly, Gail drew a breath to tell her friend and supporter about her new job and plans to leave. She would miss others at the track, but George most of all.

He spoke again before she could get a word out. "Sorry to hear that Samuel Schrock is stepping away from the Amish horse-trading business. He was a likable guy."

Gail froze. Samuel was more than likable. So much, much more. "What do you mean?"

"He came by earlier this week. Said he appreciated working with me, but he was going to leave the business. Something about going back to work with his brother making furniture."

She blinked. Samuel didn't want the furniture business. He'd hate working all day inside. His passions were horses and farming. Had Ruby made good on her threat even though Gail was staying out of the community? The words were hoarse when she finally got them out. "Did he say why he was quitting?"

George frowned. "Not exactly. Something about different priorities. I'm surprised he didn't talk with you about it."

Blood drained from Gail's face, leaving her light-headed. Was that why Samuel had called her? Sometime after reeling with emotion from her new employer's call, she listened to voice mails that'd accumulated while the phone had been off. One of them had been from Samuel, left the Monday after the barn-raising.

She'd cried when she'd heard his unusually grave voice asking her to call him. Already several days old, Gail hadn't responded to his message. She didn't know how. Too vivid was the memory of the shock and hurt on his face when she'd railed at him. She'd wanted to blame him when all he'd done was what Gail had wanted all along—reunite her with her family.

Surely he wouldn't leave everything he'd ever wanted because of her? Was that what the call had been about? Telling her he didn't want to work with her anymore? She should explain that was no longer a factor as she was leaving. She would help him find another driver. He could keep his business.

Pulling out her phone, Gail keyed up Samuel's number.

George glanced over from the notes he was making on his trotter's performance. "Hope you can catch him on that. He said he was shutting off his phone. Something about baptism."

Baptism? That ended *rumspringa*, which usually concluded when a man found a woman he wanted to marry. But who? Gail's breath caught as she thought about their time together. What if Hannah had been right? Had there been more to Samuel's attention to Gail than just his flirtatious nature?

"Oh, and I gave him my address. He didn't know yours and he said he wanted to send you something." George's voice tapered off as he focused on the track when the sound of a motor indicated another group of trotters were preparing for a trial.

Gail furrowed her brow. Samuel didn't have anything of hers to return.

Except, perhaps, her heart.

Did he even know it was his?

Why would Samuel quit the job he obviously loved?

Unless…he loved something more?

She stared down at the name on her display. Samuel Schrock. The name seemed so flat on the device compared to the vitality of the man. Her trembling fingers bumped the keyboard and a question popped up. Did she want to delete the contact? Her hand hovered over the display. Did she? Was it already too late? Gail lifted her hand to her cheek to ensure it didn't accidentally touch the phone. Her memory lingered over the precious days spent with her family. The unquestioning support they'd given her. The support he'd given her.

Although she'd dishonored them in the community by leaving, no one in her family had let her down. She'd let herself down by running away and not trusting them. Yes, Samuel had done the wrong thing for the right reasons. But he'd given her back her family.

Gail drifted several yards down the fence from George before resting her arms on the rail and staring numbly at the racing Standardbreds as they thundered by behind the moving starting gate. The horses' black legs were churning so fast, they were a blur. Churning like her thoughts.

Wasn't that like her? Always running? She'd started running because of shame and fear. And she'd been running ever since.

This new job would be continuing that unhappy path. Certainly, it would be easier financially, but they'd still be running. How long was she going to continue? What was she teaching Lily in the process?

Ja, the job opportunity was an answer to prayers. But was it the only one? Gail's fingers tightened on the slickly painted rail. Or even the right one? Without the wreck, she wouldn't have had contact with the freight business owner. She'd also not have had the precious days at home, embracing how much she'd loved the Amish life. And she wouldn't have faced Ruby and her biggest fears.

Or recognize how she felt about Samuel.

She'd been running for years. Years, filled with struggles. What would've happened if she'd walked back up the lane that day instead of leaving?

Whatever would've happened, *Gott* would've seen her through it.

Oh, the time she and Lily had missed with family! What possibilities might she be missing with Samuel if she ran again, instead of taking a chance with him?

The horses swept into the backstretch. A few lagged behind the pack. They likely wouldn't make the time trials. But what if their purpose wasn't on the track, but somewhere else? What if *Gott* wanted her purpose to be somewhere else, as well? If only she'd trust Him and stop running. Was she courageous enough to take the chance? To trust the man He'd put before her?

Samuel. Oh, Samuel.

The beating of hooves and heavy breathing indicated the horses were pounding up the homestretch and nearing the finish line. Gail's breath was racing, as well. Was it possible that *Gott* wanted her to go home? The horses flew across the finish and began slackening their pace. Gail blindly watched them, her fingers clenched on the top board. Her breath slowed at the wave of peace that swept over her at the prospect. Home…

When Gail was certain her knees would hold her, she hurriedly retraced her steps down the rail to where the trainer was again making notes.

"George, do you have a minute?"

Four Belgian draft horses lifted their huge heads and watched from the pasture as Gail drove up the lane. Her arrival was quieter with just the truck and not the rattle of the horse trailer, but Samuel must have heard it anyway. He came to the door of the barn and watched from there as she parked the truck and got out.

Fair enough. After what she'd said the last time she'd seen him, Gail wasn't surprised he didn't want to come any closer. She'd have to be the one to close the distance between them. Gail just hoped Samuel would listen when she did. She hoped she wasn't wrong this time, with this man. Chest tightening with each step, she walked over until she faced him in the afternoon shade of the big barn.

"I'm making a goodbye trip."

Samuel winced before slowly nodding, his

blue eyes uncharacteristically somber under the brim of his straw hat.

Oh, she loved those eyes. Try as she might to avoid it, Gail knew she'd started to fall that first morning in this very farmyard.

"Since you've shared some adventures, I thought you might like to say goodbye, as well."

Glancing over to the truck, Samuel inhaled deeply and nodded again. "Is she in the truck?"

"She is the truck."

Samuel looked back at her in confusion.

"I'm selling Bonnie."

"What?"

"I'm selling Bonnie. And the trailer."

"But…what are you going to do?"

From his concerned bewilderment, Gail allowed herself to hope. She smiled crookedly. "I'll still drive horses. But they'll just be in front of me instead of behind."

Samuel's brow furrowed, then his beautiful blue eyes widened. The look in them gave her courage. Stepping closer, he lifted his arms like he was going to wrap them around her, before halting a foot away with clenched fists. "But what about the Weavers and Lily?"

"They were right. It is best for an Amish

child to be raised in a two-parent home. But you were right about Bishop Weaver, as well."

Samuel shook his head in puzzlement.

"When you said he was something of a matchmaker. They had a part in bringing us together. If I hadn't confronted them, I'd never have had the courage to be your wife." Samuel didn't say anything. Gail's mouth grew dry. "If you ever get around to asking me," she added hoarsely. When he remained mute, Gail shifted her feet and slid her hands down the front of her jeans. They were as sweaty as the first time she'd met him.

"I'm hoping you were thinking about asking me. I'm hoping the way you acted and made me feel wasn't because I was just one of the many girls you've flirted with. That there was something more between us." Gail struggled to read his face, but for once, his attractive features were expressionless. What if she'd misread his actions? Her heart was hammering. "I've been wrong before when I thought a man cared for me. Oh, please don't let me be wrong this time, because what I felt for him is nothing compared to what I feel for you."

When Gail couldn't stand his stillness anymore, when she almost turned back to the truck to run again, Samuel lunged forward.

She lost her breath when he swept her into his arms.

"Oh, Gail. There's more. There's so much more. From the moment I met you and you admitted you gave a name to a piece of metal, it's been you. You and Lily. Why do you think I worked so hard to get you back into my world? Maybe my methods weren't good, but my intentions were. I thought that was what you wanted, too. Until what you said…"

Gail lifted a hand to rest it gently at his mouth, stopping his words. "Samuel, you gave me back my family. I could love you for that alone, but my heart became yours for countless other reasons. I'm so sorry I lashed out that day. I was scared. I felt guilty."

Samuel tenderly kissed her fingers. "*Nee*, I thought about what you'd said. Thought about it a lot. You were right. I called you but when I didn't hear back, I figured that you didn't want anything to do with me. So I determined I'd find a way to help you support Lily, or at least be able to keep the Weavers from her. I couldn't stand the thought of you two struggling on your own. I was going to send you money."

"I wouldn't have let you. Just like I can't let you give up your job as the Amish horse trader."

He raised his eyebrows as he lowered her to her feet. "Why?"

"Because you love it. And I love you, so I want you to be happy." Gail didn't know if she could stand without his support. She curled her free hand behind his neck. Flicking the back brim of his hat, she smiled when it slid farther down his forehead. "Besides, I'll be in the market for a horse."

Samuel dipped his head, giving her a quick kiss on the lips. When he leaned back, Gail got lost in his dazzling grin. "You know what would really make me happy?"

"What?"

"You becoming my wife. And Lily, my daughter."

Gail's heart drummed so loudly, she was surprised he didn't ask what the racket was. "By all means, let's make us both happy." She kissed his clean-shaven chin. As a married man, it wouldn't stay clean-shaven for long.

"I'm glad you realize one thing." Samuel's eyes were suddenly serious. Gail's breath caught for a moment before she noticed the glint in them. "You'll need a horse. *Gut* thing you know a *gut* horse trader."

Gail closed her eyes, relaxed in his strong arms and thanked *Gott*. "*Ja*. Very *gut* for me."

Epilogue

Gail started for the window to again look out on the snowy landscape before she caught herself, heading instead toward the stove to make more coffee. It shouldn't be too long now. As was tradition, she didn't attend church the day of publication. Hannah had offered to stay with her, but Gail had sent her sister on, leaving Gail alone at her folks' farm with Lily. As soon as the deacon announced their intention to marry, just before the last hymn, Samuel would leave church and come straight here to tell her that they'd been "published."

Gail concentrated on keeping her hand steady so she wouldn't scatter a dusting of coffee grounds all over the counter. This time, instead of that marriage announcement four years ago, her jitters were due to excitement, not shock and dismay.

As she'd left before being baptized, Gail could return to the community, but she did need to make a freewill confession to one of the district church leaders. Although it would've been easier choosing one other than the bishop, she'd talked with Ezekiel Weaver. As it was freewill, with a set face, he'd solemnly offered counsel and determined to close the issue in private, probably to protect Atlee's reputation. Gail didn't care. To the Amish, a sin confessed was a sin forgiven. Gail was finally free of her burden of guilt and shame. Free to stop running and return home. Free to love Samuel. With her pending marriage to him, free to keep Lily.

Ruby Weaver hadn't acted on her threat against Samuel. Based on the way Samuel's business had grown and the respect he obviously held in the community, if she tried now, she'd have a difficult time turning people away from him.

After several weeks of classes, Gail and Samuel had both been baptized into the church. At the end of the ceremony, as was customary, she'd received the holy kiss from the bishop's wife. Ruby's eyes had been narrowed during the awkward encounter, but with the rounding under Louisa's apron visible where Jethro's wife sat on a backless pew nearby, nothing was said.

Maybe over time, they'd see about the Weavers' interactions with Lily. Gail knew, as she was forgiven, she needed to forgive, as well. Besides, she'd learned to trust her and Lily's future to *Gott*. He did a far better job with it than she had done.

A flash of brown and black went by the window. Samuel was coming up the lane. When Gail set the coffee can on the counter with a thud, Lily, Amish outfit complete down to apron and *kapp*, skipped over to her. Gail lifted her daughter to her hip so she could see out.

"Is our Amiss man coming?"

"*Ja*, Lily." She'd been teaching Lily the language of the Amish. "Our Amish man is coming." Gail slid a hand over her forearm, smoothing down the goose bumps that rose there at the privilege of claiming Samuel. Of being claimed by him.

"I'm glad he's ours."

Gail was surprised to hear her daughter voice her own thoughts. "Why, sweetie?"

"Because he's making our family bigger. And families are important."

Gail watched Samuel draw Belle to a halt. Breath pluming in the cold November air, he swung lithely out of the buggy, secured the horse and hurried toward the house. When he saw them looking out the window, he waved, wearing the biggest smile she'd ever seen on his face. And that was saying something for him. Heart full, Gail smiled and waved in return.

"They are indeed, Lily. They are indeed."

* * * * *

*If you loved this story,
check out* The Amish Bachelor's Choice,
also by Jocelyn McClay,

And be sure to pick up:

A Summer Amish Courtship
by Emma Miller
An Amish Easter Wish
by Jo Ann Brown
The Amish Nurse's Suitor
by Carrie Lighte
The Amish Teacher's Dilemma
by Patricia Davids

*Available now from Love Inspired!
Find more great reads at
www.LoveInspired.com.*

Dear Reader,

Welcome back to Miller's Creek, a community Gail Lapp wants to return to, although she's concerned about what her welcome might be there.

I didn't start out intending to tell a tale of a prodigal daughter, but Gail took it upon herself to write her own story. She just didn't expect Samuel Schrock to disrupt it.

We all write our own stories in some way. So it's comforting, since unlike a keyboard where there are delete and escape keys to revise our narratives, no matter what we might put on our pages, God wants a happy ending for us.

Thank you for the honor of allowing me to write about the growing community of Miller's Creek. Hannah Lapp has been patient and calm as she waits for her own story. I wonder what it would take to disrupt her composure… I hope you'll join me in finding out soon.

In the meantime, you can find me on Facebook.

May God bless you,
Jocelyn McClay

ReaderService.com has a new look!

We have refreshed our website and we want to share our new look with you. Head over to ReaderService.com and check it out!

On ReaderService.com, you can:

- Try 2 free books from any series
- Access risk-free special offers
- View your account history & manage payments
- Browse the latest Bonus Bucks catalog

Don't miss out!

If you want to stay up-to-date on the latest at the Reader Service and enjoy more Harlequin content, make sure you've signed up for our monthly News & Notes email newsletter. Sign up online at ReaderService.com.